Lawf

The Sigma M...

By Marie Johnston

Lawful Claim

Copyright © 2015 by Lisa Elijah

Copyediting by EbookEditingServices.com

Second Edition Editing by The Killion Group

Cover by P and N Graphics

Agent E wasn't always an evil Sigma Agent. Even though evil had her claws in him, he couldn't help but hang on to his past and watch over the family he lost, protecting them by staying dead to them. Until one night, he interfered.

When Ana Esposito's life, and that of her son, was saved by the husband she had buried over a decade ago, her world irrevocably changed. Any chance of safety for her and her son lay with the hardened man that used to be the love of her life.

To Melissa.
I will keep paying my bestie, and favorite beta
reader, in coffee and pictures of shirtless hotties.

Chapter One

This was his favorite spot.

Leaning against an old cottonwood, the bark digging into his back, Agent E shoved his hands in his pockets and watched through the window as a pretty, curvaceous woman cleaned up the dishes after supper. She looked as good as she always did, even with her silky black hair caught up in a messy bun at the top of her head, a sign she had a shit day at work. Her old T-shirt was actually his old T-shirt.

Wonder if the suave asshole knows that? Probably not, or the shirt would have been shredded and burned. Gone, like all the pictures of her and her late husband together. E didn't like Ana Esposito's fiancé. Not at all. Nothing about the guy sat well with him. Something about the suits and the mannerisms, like the dude thought he was better than Ana and she should thank her lucky stars he took pity on her enough to be willing to marry her.

Then again, no one in E's mind was good enough for his wife, including himself. Madame G, the madwoman leading the Freemont chapter of Sigma, made sure of that. Made sure Julio Esposito died a horrid death, only to be resurrected and morphed into Sigma Agent E—expert hunter and murderer. It was better for Ana if he stayed dead, his only identity Agent E. The things Madame G had made him do, the things he still had to do to survive…

Shoving those thoughts to the back of his mind, he zeroed in on Ana, savoring every glimpse he could as she crossed the break in the curtains. One night a few months ago, he stood out there like the dumbass he was. The window was cracked open, and his enhanced hearing picked up on her fiancé talking to her about installing a new window, the kind with the blinds in the glass. Fuck, he couldn't see through plastic.

The old window still stood, and E suspected it was because Ana refused to let go of Nana's hand-sewn curtains. When Ana's grandmother had passed away, she gifted Ana with the house. E never had a chance to reside there back when he was human and married to Ana, but he was forever grateful to Nana. His demise had left Ana nearly homeless. Nana's generosity ensured she would never have to worry again.

Good luck to the suit-wearing bastard trying to get Ana to move.

A lump formed in E's throat, like it always did, at the next person to walk into the kitchen.

Tall for his age, with neatly-trimmed dark hair and coffee-brown eyes, ten-year-old Julio Jr. was the spitting image of his father. It was a rare sight of Julio and his mom together. Julio was only a few inches shorter than his petite mother, but would likely grow as tall, or taller, as E. With skin slightly darker than Ana's, but not as cocoa-hued as E's, Julio already had the swagger that would turn young women's heads in his teenage years.

But, as E's snooping had revealed, Julio had the brains of his mother. Maybe that would help him avoid what Ana termed "the hero complex," a character trait that had landed E exactly where he was now. Over ten years ago, E had rushed into a shit storm to save the day with no thought of the consequences. Had he hung back, analyzed the scene more thoroughly, maybe he would've noticed the unnatural tendencies of the fire and pondered the presence of screaming women and children in an abandoned warehouse. Maybe he would have felt the hair at the back of his neck stand on end from the malevolent force waiting for him to rush into the building before backup had arrived.

Ana stood with her hands on her lushly-rounded hips, scolding Julio for the cesspit he called a room. Gah, the boy was a slob, a result of his mother's overbearing tendencies where the boy was concerned. Had things been different, Ana would've been more laid back. She would not have had to give birth, raise a child, and finish school all on her own, after her husband was supposedly killed in the line of duty.

Headlights swung past E's hiding spot and the suit-wearing bastard pulled up. The guy didn't live with Ana, but he came by most every night. Some nights became sleepovers. E ground his teeth to a near breaking point every time he saw them kiss. When the kisses would deepen and E could see the bastard taking what should still rightfully be his, E usually had to leave. Otherwise, he might rip the tree he reclined against right out of the ground.

What a hypocrite. The games Madame G enjoyed most were making her Agents perform—in all kinds of ways. Sex was one way she broke them down, stripped them of any humanity, and of their former identity. When Agent E woke up after that fire, he found himself healed and stronger than ever. He also found he'd been shot up with a roofie on steroids and given to the seduction trainers Madame G employed.

E snorted, *trainers*. More like depraved individuals who got off on power over another's body. But it didn't matter. E had been like a lunatic, in sensory overload, didn't remember who he was, and especially didn't feel human anymore. He tore through those women and demanded more. So Madame G sent more. E spent himself on whoever was in the room and was willing.

Thank whatever power out there working against Madame G for Agent X. When E was throwing himself against the door asking for more, crazed out of his mind, a couple of vampires threw him into a room with a young recruit Madame G was trying to break.

E had stalked into the room and saw a fragile young woman, not much younger than his wife…and then it had registered. His wife. E's memories had poured back as he took in the naked form with hair as long and black as his Ana's, curled up on the floor, shaking. He had dropped to his knees, a sense of who he had been flooding his consciousness. The trembling young woman gazed at him with stunning green eyes that were a mirror to her vulnerability. Then she lunged up and attacked him.

X had damn near wrenched his head off and he didn't fight her, willed her to end him, because he had already ended everything that had mattered to him.

He cursed the hell out of her when he woke up in a sticky pool of his own blood, or what had been left after she drank from him.

"Why didn't you kill me?" he had croaked to her.

The young X, with her brilliant green eyes, met his stare. "You were able to stop yourself. So was I. Maybe you and I can be strong enough to stop *her*."

If the slip of a woman hadn't just torn out his throat, he might have failed to take her seriously. Yet the resolution in those eyes, the dead serious tone of her voice…Like she had done, he too decided his old life was gone, and he would do everything he could to ruin the monster who took it all from him.

"Who did she take from you?" E had asked her after his decision was made.

"It's who she didn't take," X had responded flatly.

And that was when E realized his vendetta wasn't about revenge. It was about saving the family left behind. Because Madame G had made it clear, not long after his introduction to X, that his family, including the baby he hadn't known he was expecting, would pay for any hint of noncompliance to Sigma's master plan, and more importantly, Madame G's master plan.

Revenge became a tricky bitch to work with.

E stood there recalling about those early days of his conversion to whatever the hell he was now. He watched the bastard—what was the asshole's name? Griffin—Griffin, the suit-wearing bastard, give Ana a peck on the cheek and take her luxurious locks down from the haphazard bun. Ana had to hate that. She loved her hair, but the weight of a healthy, full head of thick hair that fell past her shoulder blades gave her a tension headache after a stressful day at work. And when she was puttering around the house, she always wanted it out of the way.

Movement beside the house caught his attention. A shadow flitted through the trees. E narrowed his eyes, his inhuman senses picking out a kid on a bike. Julio was riding away from the house and E decided to follow him. He suspected Julio left without telling his mother, he and never went out after dark. Why tonight?

Drifting through the trees that stretched from the far side of the street to Ana's house, E kept pace with the bike, not even breathing heavily, but growing concerned as his son neared the river. Ana's house sat on the outskirts of Freemont and was situated on the border of an older development. The touch of rural meant the neighborhood was too dark for a young boy to be out alone. The river nearby was all the more reason this didn't feel right.

Sensing people in the vicinity, E slowed, moving quick enough to keep up with Julio, but scanning the area with his senses. Two people, both male, one younger. His gut tightened. None of this was good.

Julio headed toward a rocky, rugged area by the bank of the river that was often deserted, at least by anyone with good intentions. What was his son up to?

The lanky boy ditched the bike and walked toward the riverbank. E couldn't get much closer without being seen. The trees became too small and too sparse near the water. The unfamiliar tingle of nervousness arose. Damn, this wasn't good. It didn't bode well that he was nervous for his son. Nerves made for stupid decisions. Everything he'd done in the last decade had been with cold deliberation. Now wasn't the time for stupid mistakes.

"Hey," Julio called to a shadowy figure. "You got the card?"

What the fuck? Card?

"Yeah kid," the figure called. "Come on over."

No. Don't. Fuck, Julio, just don't. The bank of the river wasn't a cliff by any means, but it was a good ten to fifteen feet in the air with a solid current underneath. Nothing a seventy-five-pound ten-year-old could handle.

"Is it a Holofoil rare first edition?" Julio neared the figure standing way too close to the edge. "I've been wanting that type of Venusaur forever."

Hope filled his voice, and E couldn't figure out for the life of him what the hell his son was talking about. Was it even English?

"Yeah, right here." The other boy sounded rushed, hyped on adrenaline. "Come here."

Don't go there, Julio.

The older kid, a wiry fifteen-year-old, if that, from what E could tell, held out a small rectangular card. A trading card? Fucking figures. His son would turn away every drug dealer known to man, but dangle a Pokémon card in front of the kid's face and he epically loses all common sense. Or as much as a ten-year-old can have.

As Julio grabbed the card, the second male strode from the trees toward the boys, putting all of E's reflexes on high alert.

"Dude, this is my dad."

Julio spun around to the stranger, a look of panic on his face.

E's son took a step backward, thankfully away from the river's edge, but not nearly far enough to grant E some peace.

~12~

"You Ana's son?" the man almost demanded.

Warily looking around, Julio answered cautiously. "Yeah."

"Good." The man stepped forward, shoving both hands into Julio's chest so hard the boy didn't stagger back, but flew over the edge into the river.

No! Breathing like a bull through his nose, E closed his eyes, commanding his feet to stay right where they were set. His keen hearing picked up a splash, but no shouting from his son, which did not bode well.

Wait. It. Out.

The two peered over the edge, afraid to get too close.

"Kid?" the adult called.

As much as E wanted to hear his son's voice, he fervently hoped Julio didn't answer if he was able to.

"Come on, let's go." The teenager was bouncing up and down from foot to foot.

"Yeah, the water should take him under. There's no way he can crawl up these banks by himself." The two turned and headed toward the street where a beat-up car was parked a few blocks away.

E was already advancing toward the water's edge, aiming downstream a bit where the swift current might have carried Julio.

Peering over, he searched down the bank to where Julio would've entered the water. Nothing. Shuffling along, he followed the uneven, rocky edge when finally, his sensitive hearing picked up some coughing.

Sprinting toward the sound, a good hundred yards away, E fought branches of old, worn trees bordering the river's edge. There, a small form, almost six feet down, had gotten slapped against a rocky outcropping and was hanging on for dear life.

"Julio."

His son looked up and E despised the fear he saw in the kid's brown eyes, hated that his son would ever look at him in fear. "Hang on. I'm coming down to help you out."

His breathing choppy as water splashed him in the face, Julio looked like he contemplated swimming away. What E wouldn't give to hunt down the man who did this to his kid. But doing so would endanger little Julio's life even more if dear old dad interfered.

Quickly gauging the stability of the shore that had been cut down over the centuries by the river, E zeroed in on enough rocky outcroppings to make it down to where Julio was clinging.

"Julio," E spoke calmly, catching the boy's eye, "hang on."

Whether it was the calm certainty in E's voice or just that he didn't want to drown, Julio solemnly nodded, and he hugged the outcropping even tighter.

E slid down on his belly to the first tenuous foothold and quickly descended to water level. Trying to stay out of the water, not wanting to end the night fighting the water's pull with his load of weapons while keeping his son's head above water, E reached as far out as he could while still holding onto the slight purchase he had. He was only inches from Julio's hands.

"Can you grab onto me?"

Uncertainty plagued Julio as he considered E's extended hand. Leaning as far as he could, E could almost brush against his son's skin.

"Just grab for me. I'll catch you."

Instead of lunging forward, toward the outstretched hand, Julio made the critical mistake of loosening his grip. The pull of the water was too much for the spindly arms. Terror filled Julio's face and he drifted away.

E twisted and pressed his booted feet into the edge, using his body as a bridge. He grabbed the same outcropping Julio was holding onto and snatched his son's outstretched arm. Yanking him in, Julio yelped as E swung him closer to grab him around the side, pushed himself off the rocks, and threw his son up and over the edge. Using his enhanced strength and reflexes, E sprang up, landing next to the gasping boy. Shivers wracked his small body, and E suspected that it was more from the adrenaline and near-death experience than any real chill.

He sat down beside Julio to figure out what to do next. Pat him on the back and say, "There, there?" Shit, tonight was the first night he'd even touched his son.

Shit…tonight he'd gotten to touch his son. E let the awe sink in. Then the dread. It was imperative he remained dead to those he loved. So now what?

"You okay?"

Julio sat up in a position that mimicked E's—knees drawn in, hands wrapped around them, staring out over the river. "Yeah."

"Listen. You can't tell anyone about me. Tell your mom what happened, but you can't mention me."

Julio looked up at him, squinting like it would help him see better in the dark. The development's streetlights barely touched this far off the beaten path, and there was little moonlight to highlight his features.

"Why not?"

"It's safer for you. For us both."

Julio nodded. "All right. Why did they try to kill me?"

E ground his teeth together. "I don't know. But they might try again. Stay in public. Don't leave the house until the police figure it out."

Julio frantically shook his head. "I don't want to tell Mom. She'll kill me."

Before he could stop himself, he rubbed Julio's back. "She wants you safe. She won't be angry you told her the truth."

But dude, she'd be pissed someone hurt her son. Ana's temper was legend although she rarely unleashed it. One night he had left his dirty clothes laying around one too many times. He found his underwear on the ceiling fan, in the blinds, and had to fish one out that plugged the toilet. Even at the compound, he was still religious about using a laundry basket.

"You tell her, you hear? About all of this. Just say you climbed out yourself."

"Will you walk me home?" Julio's shivering had subsided, but he faced a dreaded deed.

E hopped up and pulled Julio to standing. "I'll follow in the tree line while you bike back. Straight home."

"Yes, sir."

E's heart swelled with pride, remembering how he used to refer to his father in the same tone. Even after he was an adult, he talked to his veteran father with nothing but respect up until a heart attack claimed the man's life.

"Let's go."

Chapter Two

Griffin Chase wandered into the kid's room. Julio was sitting with a thick book open on his lap, a dim lamp barely lighting the room.

"You did good tonight, kid."

"Thanks," Julio muttered, otherwise ignoring Griffin.

Forcing his irritation down, Griffin shoved his hands into his chino pockets so he wouldn't fist them in front of the kid.

It'd taken him hours to calm Ana down. Still, she insisted on calling the police. They came over, questioned Julio about his near-drowning incident, went to investigate the site where it had allegedly taken place, and said they'd call if they needed anything else.

"So what happened?"

Julio gave him a droll look, and Griffin's hands fisted of their own volition inside their tight constrains. Kids and attitudes didn't sit well with Griffin, and there was an overabundance of both in this house.

"I told the cops everything."

Yeah, including a too accurate description of the kid with the coveted Pokémon card and enough of a description of the man to make certain John Q. Public would be able to point the police in the right direction.

What a fucking mess.

"It's okay to tell me everything. I understand talking to the police might be a little intimidating, and you might not have mentioned everything."

Julio rolled his eyes up at Griffin, considered him for all of one second, and went back to inspecting whatever the hell the book was that sat open on his lap.

Griffin rocked on his feet waiting for Julio to add anything to the conversation, like how the hell he survived being thrown into the fucking river in the middle of the night. Following Julio's gaze, Griffin glanced down to the thick book he was paging through, surprised to see it was actually a photo album.

Griffin's jaw worked at the sight of photos of the happy couple strewn across the pages: Julio's father and Ana shortly after they met, smiling together at a picnic, hugging each other at their wedding, Julio Senior in his police uniform.

"How did you survive the river, Julio?"

"I climbed out." Julio, the little shit, repeated without looking up, riveted on a picture of his father dressed as Freemont's finest.

So that's the way it was going to be. Leaving the room, wishing he could inform the kid just how he was going to take his ire out on Ana, Griffin shut the door behind him. He had a call to make and a woman to bang senseless.

*****

"Think I hit him?" X bounced next to E as they walked from the garage in Sigma's compound into the loading bay, heading toward their quarters.

"You know you did. At least you didn't use silver this time."

X fell quiet, brushing her black hair off her forehead, her brilliant green eyes downcast. Damn, E knew that bothered her. She had quite the contentious relationship with the local Guardian commander Rhys Fitzsimmons. So when Commander Fitzsimmons and Bennett Young showed up to deal with a rogue shifter X and E had also been chasing, there were a few bullets exchanged.

E would've rather bought the rogue shifter supper for killing Agent L and Agent M. But since the shifter would soon go feral and need to be put down anyway, they set out to kill him and kill him they did. Commander Fitzsimmons almost put a bullet in E's head right as E was taking aim on the rogue, so X "distracted" him, getting grazed herself by Bennett as she nailed the commander's shooting arm. Both Bennett and X missed vital organs on purpose, but regardless, E was glad because he suspected the commander's aim would've been true, and a head wound is a bitch to recover from.

Not to mention the shit he would take if X had to carry his ass out of there.

Get up here.

Aw, shit. The mental summons from Madame G left a pounding headache behind. He subtly rubbed his temples. X didn't suffer the same effects, being a shifter and telepathy was in their nature.

"What'd you do?" X taunted, poking him in the arm.

Scowling, he ignored her, keeping his gaze on the floor as they changed direction to head to the elevator.

X grew quiet, then gazing at him speculatively asked, "Seriously E, what did you do?"

"The less you know the better." He kept silent about the other night when he had saved his son. Sure X knew he creeped around his wife's place, but if he entered Shit City as far as Madame G was concerned, X needed to keep to her own path and not go down with him.

Tension lined her face, mirroring E's own, and they silently rode the elevator up to Madame G's suite.

The chime of the elevator made E feel like this was a turning point in his life, a significant moment that he couldn't change, couldn't back away from.

The doors slid open presenting Madame G standing in her floor-length, blood-red kimono. Her hands tucked within the sleeves, the only skin showing was her porcelain face and ink-black hair pulled into a high ponytail.

Both X and E approached and stood before the evil woman, eyes downcast, heads bowed, hands clasped in front of them.

"Tell me how the hunt went?" their mistress intoned.

It was a loaded question. But for what intent, he didn't know.

"He was dispatched," X replied dutifully, her bangs falling onto her face, revealing the shaved sides. Her hair had been up in a messy faux hawk, but their little scrimmage mussed it up.

"Without incident?"

"No, Madame G. Two Guardians arrived and we engaged, but were able to take out the rogue." E hoped the bloodshed would satisfy Madame G.

No luck.

"Tell me, Agent E and Agent X, how is it you keep encountering the Guardians, yet they are still alive?"

E suppressed a shiver. Shit was starting to get real. Madame G tested their dedication to her cause periodically, but with both his and X's wit, they were able to cheat the tests and retain some semblance of humanity.

"They are highly trained fighters, Madame G," X answered first. "Our primary goal is to complete our mission, and we often don't retain the firepower afterward to dispatch the Guardians. They are armed more heavily now since we have killed one of their own."

"Hmmm." Madame G stared at them. E would kill to look up at her, read the conniving bitch's intention in those glittering, almond-shaped, black eyes, but he remained unmoving like a rock.

"Agent E, where were you two nights ago?"

Oh shit, oh shit, oh shit.

"At Happy Hari's getting a blow job, Madame G." And he had. He hated it, every second, but at least the talented ladies at the massage parlor knew how to give a happy ending to the most uptight of clients.

"Did your blow job take all night?"

"Yes, ma'am." He threw in a bit of arrogance. If he paid well enough, and he did, it took as long as he told the ladies it did. Happy Hari's had been a solid alibi for him many times.

"Mmm." He hated her wordless comments. "Your wife is getting married, I hear."

Translation: I keep tabs on her and will kill her if you deviate.

E clenched his jaw, jerking his head into a nod as if the information surprised him. Hearing the words sucked, almost as much as seeing the evidence. He didn't trust his voice not to betray his knowledge of his wife's business, and that would let Madame G know some part of him wasn't fully committed to his dark mistress.

They stood there, X and E, side-by-side, while Madame G considered them.

"Go. I'll have another mission for you tomorrow. Pack your bags, it's out of town."

The feeling of foreboding came back full force. Madame G was sending them out of town within days of his son's attack. Could it be connected, and how?

Chapter Three

Driving home, Ana Esposito groaned and repositioned herself in her seat. Griffin had been uncharacteristically rough with her in bed last night. Again.

Again, she wondered if she had made the right decision saying yes to his proposal. He was a good man and seemed to get along with Julio, at least as much as her son let any of the men she'd dated get along with him. Ana loved Griffin, but lately, he'd seemed distant, brooding, and she had been questioning that often misinterpreted emotion—love.

While she might love Griffin, she was not *in love* with him, and how pathetic was that? A good-looking man who treated her right…usually. Ana shifted again and grimaced. He tolerated her son's aloof behavior and held down a good job, yet she still carried a torch for her dead husband.

It wasn't Griffin's fault she couldn't get past her feelings for her late husband. Or at least, it wasn't his fault that she had experienced the head over heels, madly in love emotion in the past to know that what she felt for Griffin wasn't it.

But she was lonely, dammit.

For so many years, it had been her, little Julio, and Nana. Then Nana passed away after a bad bout with pneumonia and the loneliness became unbearable. Because she worked full-time and was a single mom, she had few friends she could go out with and unload her suckass day onto.

Her coworkers in the pharmaceutical lab were amazing, but not besties. There was no one she could call and vent to about the mess Julio left behind after making a snack, or how her gutters were clogged again, and she hated heights and dreaded dragging the ladder out to clean them every fall. Man, she despised that task. She could never meet coworkers after work just to relax and share in some laughs because she always had to race home to meet her son as he got off the bus.

Pulling into her driveway, she saw the bus leaving. Perfect timing. She didn't dare leave Julio alone, not after the attack three nights ago. She shivered. Griffin didn't believe Julio, but Ana was uncertain. Why would her son lie about that? "To get attention because we're getting married," Griffin had replied.

Regardless, Julio had been dripping wet and shaking when he banged on the front door that night. Ana hadn't even known he'd snuck out, or that he would ever sneak out. The police claimed there were more than Julio's footprints and everything about his story corroborated. Her heart was pounding just thinking about it.

Deep breaths. She had to calm herself before Griffin got home. He seemed to think extreme sex was the perfect way to ease her nerves. After the police had left and she'd tucked Julio into bed with the worn, ever-comforting photo album, she went to bed and tried to sleep. Griffin had come to her.

She had wanted the lights turned off, but he left them on and descended on her, despite her protests that she most definitely wasn't in the mood. "You're too wound up to sleep, let me relax you," he had said. It wasn't unpleasant, but it was definitely more vigorous than usual.

Then the next night, he took her in the shower after Julio was put to bed. Griffin's dark eyes had focused on her while he took his release; it was…disconcerting. She didn't feel the normal connection he strove to make with her in bed.

Then last night…she shifted in her seat again. When the hell did he get the idea that she liked to be spanked? Was he into that shit? If so, she should know before they tied the knot, because for her, a sore ass the next day wasn't her gig.

She pulled into the garage and waited until her son walked inside before shutting the garage door.

"Hey kiddo. How was your day?"

Julio shrugged one bony shoulder, playing with his backpack's straps. "Fine."

All right then. Sometimes, he talked nonstop about his day. Sometimes, it was "fine."

She followed him up to the door into the house and waited for him to go inside. She stepped into the entryway off to the side of the kitchen. Shoving her keys into her purse, she bumped into Julio's back, not noticing he'd stopped in his tracks.

"Whoa, sorry hon, I—" As Ana glanced up at Julio, she caught sight of what, or rather who, had made him stop short.

Two men in dark suits were facing them, silently waiting in the kitchen.

One man stepped forward, presenting a holder containing a badge of some sort, but she was too far away to see the credentials clearly. "Ma'am, we don't mean to alarm you, but you and your son are in danger."

"What? Why?" Ana's heart pounded. Who wanted to hurt her son? He was a good, sweet kid. Kids don't have enemies. And cops don't wait for you inside your home, keeping their badges too far away to see clearly.

"I'm sorry, ma'am. We need to take you with us now."

"Oh my God. What's going on? Do we have to go into witness protection or something? Did we see something we shouldn't have?" Ana kept shooting off rapid-fire questions while shoving Julio solidly behind her. Making sure her voice sounded panicked, rising in frequency, she prayed it threw the men off.

"Ma'am don't panic." One of the males clasped her arm. Meanwhile, the other male reached into his suit jacket. "The boy is in trouble; you need to come with us."

Ana nodded woodenly, her gaze on the hand on her arm, then drifting past it to his other hand, which was now holding a gun. Turning to look behind her and catch Julio's terrified gaze, she said, "Don't worry, little Pikachu, it's going to be okay."

Understanding dawned in Julio's dark eyes, to be replaced with determination. Good, he was ready.

She turned back to face the man who had a hold of her. He was on the shorter end of average, and plain in every way, but there was a gleam in his eyes…A dispassionate, almost cruel aura exuded from the man. It was the same with the taller one who, thank her lucky stars, had his back to her and was walking away toward the backdoor, probably to a nondescript, windowless van. These two men would garner no second glances if you were passing them on the sidewalk, until you looked into their eyes.

"Are you sure I can't grab a change of clothes before we go?" Ana asked.

Irritation flashed through the first man's features and as he was shaking his head. Ana steeled herself, snatching for the gun held halfheartedly in her direction. Fully utilizing the element of surprise, she jerked her arm free of his grasp and shoved her shoulder into him as her hand gripped the cool metal of the black gun. Startled, he stumbled back.

"Go, Julio!" She aimed the gun, a Glock if she had to guess, and pumped two into the man's chest before he could recover.

As Julio dashed down the hall, the man she had shot slumped to the kitchen floor. Ana took aim at the second man who was spinning in her direction, his own gun raised. Ana pulled the trigger quickly once, readjusted, and rapidly squeezed off two more shots. One to the head, two to the chest, just like her late police officer husband had taught her.

The second man was still falling to the floor when Ana sprinted down the hall, following the direction her son had taken.

Julio was standing in the doorway, waiting to see if it was his mother was coming after him, or if the men were, before he would slam the door shut and lock it. He peered past her to see if she was being followed, then backed into the room to shut and lock the door behind her. Ana raced into the room to the little safe tucked into the top of her closet.

"Are there any more of them?" Julio asked, after he got the door locked.

Oh, shit. Were there more of them? And did they hear the gunshots? "I don't know. We'll have to be extra cautious when we climb out the window." With shaking hands, Ana managed to get the safe unlocked with the key she'd hidden at the other end of the closet. "I'm proud of you, Julio. Except for not locking yourself in immediately, you did awesome, kept your cool."

Leveling him with a calm stare that camouflaged the terror racing through her, his own panic decreased a couple of levels, and he gulped before nodding calmly at her acknowledgment. This situation, whatever it was, would be hard enough to survive if either she or her son lost their shit. If she could keep herself from flying apart, then maybe her child, after all he'd been through, could make it without a nervous breakdown.

She strapped on the belt that held her husband's old duty pistol and nabbed everything from the safe: handcuffs, extra ammunition, mace. Stuffing them into the belt that barely stayed on her feminine hips, she mused at how foolish she'd felt over the years caring for these items. Up until recently, she even went to the shooting range at least once a year to stay proficient in their use. It had seemed like a disservice to let the items sit and remain unused. But the truth was, when she would look at them, she could see images of a shirtless Julio Senior, sporting a chiseled chest and a washboard stomach, sitting on the couch after a long shift. He'd chat with her about his day, idly cleaning and polishing the leather and metal that made up the various tactical gear.

He had loved his job and had taken every bit of it seriously, even teaching Ana how to clean and maintain the gun and design emergency plans in case of a fire, or God-forbid, an invasion. Wistfully, Ana wished she could give her deceased spouse a hug and a thank you, because she kept those disciplined plans in mind. As soon as her son was old enough, they talked and trained on various scenarios, and decided on a code word. Originally intended for their "in case a stranger tries to con you into going with him" plan, "Pikachu" worked, beautifully to communicate to her clever child that something was wrong and he needed to follow their escape plan. This included exiting through her home office to arm herself with protection before they climbed out the window.

"Come on." She crept up to the window with Julio glued behind her and tucked the curtain back slightly to look around outside. Seeing nothing, she tried to recall every detail from when she had pulled up to her house. "Do you remember seeing any unusual vehicles when the bus dropped you off?"

"Yeah, there was a van parked by Mrs. Mills' place. It looked like a work van, and I thought it was weird because they do everything themselves."

Pride swelled in her. She and Julio had occasionally butted heads in the past, and more frequently as he grew older, but he was an intelligent kid and took after his dad with his acute awareness of his surroundings. "Okay, we get out the window and head through the neighbors' backyards to get to the woods. We can make our way to a gas station and call for help."

"Those men weren't cops." It was statement, not a question.

"No, not of any sort." Other than the sick feeling the men gave her, everything about them screamed criminal. While their clothing and gear said they came from some organization, it was clear it wasn't a good one. The other evidence, they had broken into her house and didn't offer much of identification or explanation, which supported the evil that permeated the air in her kitchen.

Lifting the window panel out and setting it on the floor, she popped off the screen, extremely grateful she had made sure to practice window exits in case of a fire.

"I'm going to help you down. When you hit the ground, get behind the shrub in case someone is watching for us."

Her heart thudded in her ribs, waiting for a shout or pop of gunfire, as she lowered Julio to the ground. A low groan could be heard filtering down the hallway. Ana almost let out a yelp and dropped her son, but held on, and as soon as he cleared the landing, she climbed out herself. Those men should be dead; her aim was true. How could they be making noise of any kind?

No sirens could be heard. All her neighbors were still at work, and any gunfire heard by latchkey kids waiting at home would've been mistaken for TV or video games. Holding Julio's hand, she dragged him behind her as they cut across her yard and into the adjacent neighbor's yard. There would be no going back to see if the men were really dead or making sure they were. In case there were more, or the wounds weren't fatal, she and Julio needed to put the burners on and get gone.

As they ran, Ana didn't let go of Julio's hand, and made sure she kept a pace he could maintain. Her mind planned their next move. There was a gas station over a mile away where they could use a phone. She could use her cell phone, but since the men were in her house, did they monitor her cell? It sounded far-fetched, but this morning, so did an abduction. Why would they want her and her son?

"Mom," Julio huffed after they cleared one yard's chain link fence. "Do you think Dad will come save us?"

Ana's brows crinkled in surprise. "We can call Griffin after we call the police." She didn't think her son had let Griffin in enough to think of him as "Dad."

"No," Julio pressed, "*Dad*, not Griffin."

The distain that dripped off his voice when he spoke her fiancé's name did not go unnoticed, but confusion overruled her dismay that her son really did hate the man she planned to marry. "What do you mean?"

They'd slowed, both of them checking for suspicious people, both having their nerves stretched razor-thin thinking they would be chased any minute. Soon they would clear the houses and could take to the trees to follow the main road to a telephone.

"You know. *Dad*." Julio stressed again, like it was so obvious. "He saved me from the river."

A chill settled into Ana's bones. What had happened to Julio that night to make him think his dad had helped him out of the river? She'd never really thought of the afterlife and what was possible. But say there were ghosts and shit. Her husband had died before Ana could tell him the good news. Julio Senior didn't know he was having a junior before he died.

Julio Senior had been working the night shift when she came home from school and took the pregnancy test. They hadn't been trying to conceive, were waiting for her to be done with school, but life had its own plan and that night there was an extra line on the testing stick that explained why she'd been so tired and cranky.

That night she had all kinds of plans running through her mind. Should she put a bun in the oven and let her husband guess at the innuendo, or just tell him outright? Then the dreaded knock on the door came. Her heart in the pit of her stomach, she opened the door to Julio's police chief and shift sergeant, and she knew, *knew*, she'd lost her best friend and lover.

"I know what you're going to say, Mom." Julio broke in before Ana could remind him that his father died well before he was born. "But I *swear* it was him. I mean, I couldn't see him very well in the dark, but he sounded just like I'd imagined and looked just like all the photos we have. 'Cept maybe a little older looking, a little sad."

Ana chose not to say anything until they cleared the houses and could hide behind a nice, big cottonwood. Then she pulled her son to face her, hands on his shoulders. "Tell me exactly what happened that night."

"It's just like I told you, but a guy came to help me out of the river, made me swear not to tell anyone about him. I know it was Dad."

"Honey, it couldn't have been your father."

Julio stared down, sadness blanketing his expression. "I didn't tell you cuz I knew you wouldn't believe me."

Of course she didn't believe him. His father had been dead for over ten years, burned so badly they couldn't have an open casket; forensics used the massive amounts of his blood at the scene that hadn't turned to ash to confirm his identity. It'd taken her hours and hours to clean the grit out of his gear once it was returned back to her, but doing so helped her feel close to him. It was something to hold onto because he'd been taken away from her decades too soon.

"Are you sure this man was real and not imagined?" Either her son's mind conjured a savior during a dire time or some Good Samaritan helped her son and wanted to remain anonymous. Maybe a homeless guy had come to his rescue?

"Mom." Julio rolled his eyes and looked at her like he did when she asked if he was sure he brushed his teeth and hair before heading out for school. He always did, but the mom in her couldn't keep from asking.

Ana decided to table the mystery man discussion for now and concentrate on survival. She clutched his hand and pulled him deeper into the trees.

Chapter Four

"**Y**ou'd better fix this," Madame G hissed into Agent G's ear, as he was forced to his knees. An unknown force cut off his air supply, and he gaped like a hooked fish. Barely able to nod, he managed to move his head enough for her to see that her words were absolutely crystal.

Sucking in a new, sweet breath, Agent G tried not to collapse and claw at his throat for the invisible vice that had been locked onto his windpipe, waiting to crush it at her command.

Agent G knew his ass was toast as soon as her cool voice had invaded his mind, summoning him to her suite at the compound. He had been commanded to stay far away from Sigma's Freemont sprawl as he carried out his mission, and what a mission it was. Sure, he traded some power and influence for his sweet gig, but he was still alive and had a shit-ton of authority, all while carrying out Madame G's vision of dominating the entirety of shifterkind. And he still kicked back with a cognac every night, instead of answering to some other arrogant Agent.

"My apologies, Madame G." It was dangerous to apologize to the dark mistress. It showed weakness, but he needed to stress that the epic fuck-up was not his fault. Not this time. "Agent H and Agent I assumed the kid would come home and be alone for a few minutes while Ana ran late like normal. Then they could use him to get Ana to come without a fight."

Air was forced out of Agent G so fast that he flew forward and nearly kissed the floor hard enough to lose some teeth. Catching himself with a sharp jar to his arm, he tried to suck in air, his gut caved like a heavily-booted foot had just kicked him. All this, without Madame G laying one finger on him.

"And why is that Agent G?" Her rage seethed. "Could it be because you thought to dispose of the kid without having my express orders to do so? Did you not think the Esposito woman wouldn't keep a closer eye on the boy after that?"

Yeah, he should've thought of that. Should've realized Ana would deviate from her normal routine for a while until she felt Julio was safe again. But he'd been so panicked after his last confrontation with Madame G. The one where he thought to boost his standing with her and reveal to her that he thought Agent E had interacted with his family, that he was maybe not the utterly committed Agent she had molded him into.

Instead, she had been livid, and Agent G felt pain unlike any he'd ever known before, and that included his transition to Agent status. The agony was as if he burned from the inside out while someone repeatedly kicked him the nuts.

"I have plans for that boy," she had said through clenched teeth. She'd stalked in front of him as he'd writhed on the ground in pain, bleeding from his ears and nose. Then she abruptly faced him and had given her orders. "Bring the kid in. Bring them both in."

Agent G had been sent with specific instructions for when to snatch Julio and Ana and ran off with his tail between his legs. Everything was going as planned until he couldn't reach either Agent H or Agent I by radio. Then he went to the house and found them reanimating, thanks to whatever shit Madame used making them into Agents. At least until Agent G had found them, shot them each in the head again, and sawed their heads off with Ana's dull-ass butcher knife.

Breath whooshed back into his lungs, and he almost collapsed again at the relief. "I'll bring them in as you command."

"Yes. You will. And if you fail again, you will know pain and a death unlike any I have ever doled out before." The coolness of her voice was back and that was a nasty sign. If he had any chance to redeem himself at all, it would be through Ana and Julio, and whatever Madame G had planned for them.

*****

Rhys Fitzsimmons stared at the photo on his computer. A pathetic activity he found himself doing every time he sat at his desk.

Dani had enlarged it and cropped out the other teens, leaving only her, and sent it to him. He wasn't lusting over the female, that'd be sick. She was what, maybe all of seventeen in the pic? But he just couldn't *not* look at it. She was so youthful, so happy, grinning, holding a shovel from some do-gooder project all the teens in the photo had helped with.

She was listed as Alexandria King. Sarah Young, Bennett's mate, claimed her as an aunt. She was previously thought to have been killed by Madame G in her intrepid hunt for a specific vampire-shifter hybrid. Madame G then ruthlessly hunted Sarah, incorrectly informed that Sarah was the hybrid, and not Alexandria, the female they knew as Agent X.

Rhys' mind worked over that knowledge. Sometimes the jagged scar along his side throbbed. The one where Agent X had knifed him with a blade lined with pure silver. No one ever got that close to him, but his first scent of her had taken him off guard. At which point, she properly stuck him like last year's turkey and yanked down. Rhys thought he was going to cough out his liver after that, and sometimes when it rained, it still bugged him, sending achy tendrils through his side.

'Course back then, all they had were themselves to patch each other up. Now they had a sort of doctor, Garreth, and the mending was done a bit more competently, and with a steadier hand than a hyped Guardian who was pissed as hell, wanting revenge.

The knife hadn't hit his liver, but was close. It hadn't penetrated as deeply as it could've, and for the most part, he had mended completely. At least where it counted. Wasn't that the theme of his interactions with Agent X? Almost. Nearly. Close, but not critical. It wasn't too long ago that he began to suspect Agent X was more than a diabolical Sigma drone. That maybe she was after a different endgame than Madame G. But it could be wishful thinking.

Except, when he looked at a vibrant Alexandria, her brilliant green eyes alive with joy, not a care in the world other than hanging with the other honor students, he wondered, what if?

What if she weren't employed by the most evil organization known to his people, under its most vicious, evil leader? What if she had been allowed to live in a world where bad things didn't happen to good people?

Bad things. And that's why he couldn't quit staring at the picture. The young girl, so alive, so brilliant…Yet he knew what she would have been forced to endure once held in Madame G's clutches. All of her innocence—stripped. All of her optimism—destroyed. Her life—no longer her own.

He suspected the Agent he couldn't quit obsessing over still fought the good fight. If she didn't, and she had to be destroyed? Rhys shook his head, scrubbing his face with his hand and clicked his screen off.

*****

"What's doing, Biggie? You're acting like a virgin heading to her first prom with the captain of the football team." X had called him Biggie since the first day they met.

She was inspecting him as they drove back to Freemont, their mission having been wrapped up extra quickly thanks to E. It was supposed to have been an overnighter and although he and X had many slumber parties in the car because hotels were out of the question, E made quick work of interrogating the shifter spy so they could head back. In fact, he was damn near merciless, so much so that X had intervened before the spy stalled himself into a beheading. It was a bullshit mission about a shifter colony that not even Madame G gave a shit about, one that was just being monitored per Sigma's orders.

"Are you saying I'm agitated, X?"

"Not at all, Biggie. I think you're worried I'm going to pop your cherry."

E's lips quirked despite the raw feeling of foreboding he'd had for days. Considering the emotions he and X normally existed under, the foreboding had nearly driven him insane. Training his eyes back on the road, he considered, for like the hundredth time since he'd rescued his son, what to tell X.

Let's just lay it out there. "A few nights ago, I saved Julio from some thugs who tried to drown him, and I think Madame G found out. I think that's why she sent us on this insignificant assignment. I'm worried she's planning something for my family."

It wasn't often X was speechless, and from the way she was blinking at him, he'd just blown her away. He knew her too well: she wouldn't panic, she wouldn't question him ceaselessly, she wouldn't demand the entire story.

"Drop me off before you turn off to the compound, and I'll run back while you go check on Ana and Julio. If anyone asks, you kicked me out and didn't tell me why. And I'm fucking pissed about it, by the way, *and* all of your secrecy." X had his back and the less she knew, the better.

E's jaw clenched, and he pressed harder on the gas. They were finally on roads that Sigma paid good money to some very corrupt officials to not be patrolled very well. His mind worked through the deep shit he might possibly be in.

"Who do you think saw you or figured out that you helped Julio?"

E shook his head. "No clue." He ran through that night with X, and she stared out the car window for a minute.

"And the list of suspects of who might want Julio dead *and* who Julio could tell about the unknown man that saved him is?" X crossed her arms, turning her head with an eyebrow cocked, and E knew she had come to the same conclusion as him. It was preposterous, should be an outrageous assumption—but yet here he was, with his female wolf-shifter partner, hunting other wolf-shifters, for a bunch of humans and vampires. So yeah, preposterous happened.

"Exactly."

Chapter Five

"**M**om, your phone's ringing again."
"Yes, Julio." Ana tried to remain
patient. Her damn phone wouldn't stop ringing. As
much as she hated making Griffin worry, she just
didn't trust that her phone hadn't been somehow
tampered with. Not after finding men in her house,
even though her phone never left her side. But they
were in her house! What if they'd been there
before? Or, dammit, what if all those spy shows
weren't so far-fetched and they could still find her
just knowing her phone number?

Yet, she couldn't shut the damn thing off
because her city girl senses were worth shit in the
woods. It should only be one or two miles to the
nearest gas station, but staying out of sight in the
trees meant she also couldn't see where they were
going. Cue downloading a compass app so they
wouldn't walk as far off as the river. Again.

"Are we there yet?"

Ana suppressed a sigh and thought to herself,
Does it look like we're there yet? They were both
tired, hungry, and scared, and it would not make the
situation better if she bit Julio's head off, especially
since she had almost lost him twice in the last week.

Tears burned the back of her eyes. Who would do this to her sweet little boy? Sure, with her, he could cop an attitude, be insolent, and frankly disregard her orders to clean his room. But according to his teachers, he was a quiet, introspective, intelligent young man who stayed away from the drama schoolboys can create and joined in any trading card game he could.

"Mom, do you hear that? Maybe it's Dad."

Ana cocked her head and stopped walking, Julio halting next to her, her heart breaking just a little at his hopes that it would ever be his father's voice.

Then, a faint, "Ana!"

"Griffin!" She turned toward the sound, pulling Julio with her, ignoring the disappointed sound he made.

"Do you think it's a good idea? The way he's hollering, maybe the bad guys will just follow him."

While Julio had a point, Ana would feel better with another person protecting them. "We'll just follow his voice, but don't shout back." It sounded as if Griffin was near a stretch of road that turned off the main road for parking to hike the river trails.

Nearly dragging her son behind her, Ana forced herself to slow down so she wouldn't cause them to face plant into the ground. It was hard enough for her to remain upright, crossing the uneven ground in her pumps and dress pants.

They continued on until she could finally see her fiancé stomping through the trees, not far from the rugged parking area. "Griffin!" she whisper-yelled.

"Ana! My word, honey, you had me worried." His long legs ate up the ground between them. His eyes flicked to Julio and back to Ana, only concern highlighting his features.

As he wrapped his arms around her, she gave him a half hug, easing into his comfort. Her other arm remained draped over her son, unwilling to let him go now that they had to be in public to get help.

Griffin abruptly turned, assessing the gear she wore with an odd look, and clasped her free hand to pull her along behind him. "I was frantic after I got home and found the bodies. I called the police and left to search for you when you wouldn't answer your phone."

Ana had to trot to keep up with the much taller Griffin. Ana was only five-two and struggled to keep up with Griffin's long strides over the bumpy ground. From the tugging on her hand, it was apparent Julio was having difficulty, too.

As they neared the parking area, Ana craned her neck around Griffin's back to check out who, if anyone, was there. "Wait, Griffin, let's slow down. What if there's more bad guys out there and they followed you."

Stumbling into the gravel lot, Griffin pulled them along, ignoring her concern.

Ana yanked her hand free, growing alarmed. "Griffin, stop!"

There were two other vehicles next to Griffin's car. Both were black with dark windows and made the hair on the back of her neck stand on end.

"Dad!" At Julio's jubilant exclamation, Ana jerked her gaze away from the cars to a figure strolling out from between the two dark vehicles.

Time slowed. Then stopped. Ana's heart damn near stopped with it. Standing tall, holding a gun trained on Griffin, wearing all black and more weapons than she could identify, was a shockingly gorgeous, menacing version of her dead husband.

Fuck.

Just fuck.

His conspiracy theory was spot on. "You heard the lady, Griffin. Stop."

Griffin's cultured face pulled back into a sneer. "Agent E. How nice of you to look after your wife and kid. Did you get to see me banging her?"

E's jaw clenched, refusing to react to the bastard. He heard Ana's sharp inhale and in his periphery, she looked extremely pale and utterly shocked. Well, it wasn't every day a dead husband appeared, alive and well.

"Let me guess, asswipe. Agent G?"

A slow grin spread across Griffin's face and it was all E could do to not shoot him where he stood. But not in front of Julio. Besides, he needed information.

Griffin raised his arms out to the side. "The one and only. Madame G doesn't completely trust you.

She thought having someone close and personal with your wife, someone who could alert her to any interference from you, would behoove her. And what do you know?" Again with the smug grin.

"No, I don't know." E's gaze didn't move off of Griffin, but with his sharp eyesight he could see Ana hadn't moved, only held Julio close to her side.

"I didn't want the kid around after I married Ana," Griffin said flatly. "Except he came back from his dip in the river completely fine, then I found him looking at old photos of dear old dad. I put in a call to the madam, and she wants both of them. Now." Agent G gave a little shrug. "Too bad. I would've liked another night like last night. Isn't that right, darling?"

E wanted to rip the sneer off Agent G's face and tear the gleam out of those fathomless eyes when he leered back at Ana. She paled even further, swallowing hard, and glanced back and forth between the two Agents.

Agent G turned his arrogance back on E. "I have two Agents with weapons trained on her and the kid as we speak."

Holding his gun steady, E stared down the Agent. "No you don't. Their bodies are stuffed in the trunk of their car."

Shock widened the male's eyes before he turned into a blur. Shit, he was on the move. E had enough time to bring his weapon down and move his hands into a defensive position before impact.

A slash seared across his side as Agent G attacked. Instead of knocking the Agent's force back, E hugged the male closer before he could use his unnatural speed to jump away. He brought his knee up in two quick thrusts, then slammed his elbow down onto Agent G's spine. Grunts of pain rewarded E's efforts, and with one more elbow jab, E shoved the Agent to the ground, took aim, and emptied his clip into the body.

Agent G went still; everything went still. E knew he'd have to deal with the body soon, but he forced himself to look at Ana.

Soft brown eyes wide, Julio's faced buried in her shoulder, she stood shaking, starting from the devastation of her fiancé to E.

"Ana," there was no sugarcoating anything, it was only going to get worse for her, "I need to decapitate this man, or he'll keep trying to get you." Incredulous terror, that's what he would call her expression. "Then you and Julio need to come with me so I can take you to a safe place." She didn't say anything, just stayed unmoving as a statue. Julio glanced at where Agent G lay, then back up to E. "Okay? So just wait right there and don't look."

E hesitated a moment to see if Ana would do anything, or hell, move at all, but she didn't. Julio didn't glance away until E gave him a stern look. Bending down, he grabbed a leg and an arm, and hefted Agent G over to the car the Agent had arrived in. Finding the car keys, he popped the trunk and lifted the body in. Sliding his knife out of its holster, he sawed off the male's head, then dug out his Zippo. He lit the Agent's clothes on fire before opening the trunk of the car next to it, and lighting the clothes of the two Agents he'd surprised before Griffin had arrived. Beheading or burning would've been sufficient, but E didn't want to chance a passerby putting out the fire before it did enough damage. Once all the bodies were burning adequately, he turned to his wife and kid.

She still hadn't moved, except to cup Julio's head to her shoulder so he wouldn't witness any more carnage. Making a quick decision, E made his way toward the two people that were his only reason for surviving.

Ana stiffened, swallowing hard, watching him approach. He slowed the closer he got, until he stopped a foot away. "Ana, I need to get you two to safety."

Gazing deep into the eyes he used to use to center his world, even his acute senses barely registered her hand rising, and he didn't see the full-arm slap coming until his head was whipping to the side.

He looked like her husband. He sounded like her husband. He was as tall as Julio Senior had been. But what kind of bastard would let his wife think he was dead? What kind of asshole would leave a wife who was pregnant? Yes, her Julio hadn't known they were expecting before he died, or supposedly died, but he obviously knew now.

When her not-so-dead husband brought his head back around and shook off her slap, he didn't look pissed, he didn't look irritated. He looked even sadder than before.

"Let's get one thing straight, Ana. The man you were married to *is* dead. He was killed that night and turned into me. And you wouldn't want the thing I am now."

What. The fuck. Was he saying?

"Come on," his voice barely above a whisper. "The smoke will attract attention soon. We need to go."

What else could she do? Her fiancé sure sounded like he was a fraud, there were men after her and her son, and her formerly-dead husband claimed he could help them. Before she made a move to the remaining vehicle in the lot she assumed was, *what did Griffin call him?* Agent E's, Julio jerked away from her and threw his arms around the man who was once the epic love of her life.

Shock flew over Agent E's features before settling into complete stillness with his arms raised slightly above the boy's shoulders, like he was unsure of what he should do.

"We need to go," he repeated gruffly. Ana gently pulled Julio away, her heart breaking at the look of utter adoration on her son's face. This Agent E was right. Whoever the man she married had been, this was no longer that man.

Julio Senior opened a door—Ana shook that thought clear. No, *Agent E* opened a door to the third car in the gravel lot, and she climbed into the back with Julio, adjusting the armed belt around her waist. He'd better not ask for it back; she was keeping it.

He glanced down at it, recognition registering. "You promise not to shoot me?"

"No. But I won't while you're driving."

He must've believed her because he closed the door and went around to the driver's side. As they pulled away from the other two vehicles that had smoke billowing out of their trunks, she studied the man driving.

"Start talking."

His jaw muscles clenched and flexed. "Everything I tell you is going to sound absurd, like some shit out of a movie. But it's not. It's all real. The sooner you believe it, the better you'll be able to protect yourself and Julio."

She had so many questions, but she forced herself to nod and stay quiet.

"All right. From the beginning, here it is. I went to a call that night. A warehouse fire. I rushed in, only it was a setup. See, there's this secret organization called Sigma, and it's led by this madwoman, she's fuck—" He glanced back at Julio who was intently listening with his young ears. "Sorry. She's evil. I mean, literally, evil. And somehow she saw me working and decided to take me."

Okay, it was starting to get weird. "So, some evil woman faked your death so she could keep you?" Where was she and how quickly could Ana kill her? Jealously curdled her gut. Had he been with a woman this whole time?

"I can sense your anger. Just listen. There's two other species in this world besides humans: people who can shift into wolves and vampires."

"*What?*" Yes, he said to just listen, but she couldn't help it.

"Cool." This from Julio.

"Some can be, kid. But like humans, there are some who are completely evil. Sigma wants to control shifters, or wipe them out, depending on who you're following. A lot of vampires are at the head of Sigma and one of the worst is Madame G. She wants full control; I think of both species. So she faked my death, pumped me full of a special cocktail that turned me into sort of a vampire and shifter-like creature, and forced me to work for her. Otherwise, she'd hurt you or Julio."

"I buried you."

"You buried the burnt up bones of some poor homeless guy."

"They tested the blood at the scene as yours," she pointed out.

"Yeah, I lost a lot that night, fighting them. But they eventually knocked me out, put my gear and clothing on that other guy, and let him burn."

She'd been crying at someone else's grave every year? "And at no point could you get away?"

She couldn't help the scorn that slipped out. Didn't he know what she'd been through?

Silence. More jaw flexing. "After I woke up the first time, I was…" His knuckles whitened on the steering wheel, and she couldn't help but notice biceps flexing that were way bigger than his muscular frame from almost eleven years ago. "It was…I was…out of my mind. With lust." Ana's stomach bottomed out, dreading the rest. "Madame G prefers to dominate the mind through the body, and she knew I wouldn't return to you. Not after what I did, who I did."

He kept his eyes on the road, not chancing meeting her gaze in the rearview mirror. "After all the drugs wore off and my enhancements settled in, she told me that if I didn't become a loyal Agent of Sigma and follow her, she would capture you. Turn you into one of the…" Again he looked back at Julio. "There are some unfortunate women at the compound. Then she told me you were pregnant. And I knew my old life was over and I had to do whatever I could to protect you two."

Tears welled up in Ana's eyes. He sounded so…so empty. Here they sat, reunited after more than ten years of thinking that the other was completely lost to them, only to be reminded how true that was.

"So now you're Agent E?" He gave a curt nod. "And what do you do?"

"I hunt shifters mostly. And some vampires that go against Sigma's ideals."

"And you kill them?" She couldn't get out of her mind how quickly he'd put down Griffin. She saw her fiancé, rather ex-fiancé, disappear, and then he was on the ground, dead before she could blink.

"Yes."

"Are they innocents?"

The jaw muscle started ticking again. This was a new habit he'd developed, just another sign that he was a different man than Julio Senior. "Sometimes." This time he met her eyes in the rearview mirror, then glanced down to Julio. "I try not to hurt people who don't deserve it."

"Why did you…" How could Ana phrase it with a ten-year-old boy in the car? "…do what you did to Griffin?"

"Griffin was an Agent. Our identities are wiped and we are only an assigned letter. As you could probably tell, he was enhanced like me, with unnatural speed, acute senses, extra strength. It also means rapid healing. We become similar to the other species. Burning is best, but I like to make sure they can't save themselves from the fire."

"I heard the men who attacked us in my house groan after I shot them. I could've sworn I'd killed them." This was unreal. Not only did she kill two men today, but they weren't dead anymore. Just like her husband.

"Your *fiancé*," he spit out the word, "took care of them. I found them shortly after he did, and I followed him. He went back to our compound and when he came out he was beat to hell, and I continued following him. Knew he'd be looking for you."

"Where was he going to take us? Back to that compound you keep mentioning?"

"Yes."

"So where are you taking us?"

Chapter Six

L *et's do this.* "I know you're out there."
Ana pulled Julio in closer to her as the boy
was looking all around him in awe. Yeah, it was
pretty, even in the fading light. E had never been
this up close and personal. He could have gotten
close anytime, but the Guardians didn't need to
know that.

The giant log lodge they stood in front of was a
work of art, rustic art, but beautiful nonetheless.
Settled into the woods, like the trees carved it for
themselves, it was visible only due to its size.
Large, no doubt bulletproof windows, reflected the
leafy growth back, giving the massive dwelling a
natural camouflage.

"Look, I made it through all your damn hoodoo
security measures. Let's talk." Silence answered E
and he wanted to scream. He couldn't blame them
for playing the wait-and-see game, but dammit, not
now. "I need your help."

A derisive snort from the trees answered his
admission. Turning to face the woods, he didn't
have to search the trees hard to find the snort. His
wife and kid would never see them, but E could
point to exactly where each Guardian was lurking.

Please don't be in wolf form. He was already raw from years of watching Ana date and damn near get married. He didn't need her presented with a bunch of quality male flesh when they transitioned back to their human form. Call him superficial.

"I know you don't believe me, Bennett," he aimed that toward the shifter who had scoffed, "but at least hear me out."

Again, no movement. Fuckers were probably mind-speaking to each other about what to do. What a handy talent. E tried not to be jealous. Instead, he had a spendy phone plan so he and X could talk without Madame G tapping their line. Not that she couldn't, but it'd be a given if he used a company phone. And besides, he liked his gaming apps.

"Why don't you lay it all out there before we roll out the welcome mat?" This from Commander Rhys Fitzsimmons. It was a good sign, real good, that he was curious enough to hear E's story. Their history together was peppered, usually with bullet holes.

"And put your hands up while you're at it." Bennett could be a real dick.

E raised his hands in a show of deference.

"All of you."

E ground his jaw together and Ana pulled their son in tighter. "They're innocent and unarmed."

"'Scuse me if we don't take your word for it." Bennett strode into view, thankfully dressed in standard black tactical gear, strapped head to toe in weapons, gun in hand, but not aimed at his family.

A moment of gratitude swept through E. Surely the commander, and the other three Guardians out there, had their sights set on the group of three, camping out on the lodge's doorstep.

Leaning his head down, he murmured softly. "'Sall right."

Ana slowly disengaged from her son and raised her hands only slightly, keeping them at the ready to grab Julio and run if necessary. His boy, on the other hand, shoved his hands in the air, looking over Bennett like he was the newest action figure to get all fan-boy over.

"Talk," Bennett ordered, stopping several yards away.

A small gasp from Ana and a breathy "cooool" from Julio told E they saw Commander Fitzsimmons and Kaitlyn emerge from the trees, holding their weapons not quite at the ready, like Bennett.

"This is my wife and kid."

"Bullshit." Of course Bennett wouldn't believe him.

"The fuck you say?" That one from Mercury who was still in the trees.

"Whaaaat?" Kaitlyn sounded intrigued.

Only the commander remained silent, interest barely highlighting his eyes.

"Was my wife." E felt Ana's eyes drop to the ground and close in regret. *Yeah, baby, there's a lot of regret to go around.* "Madame G...picks...certain Agents. Hand-selects them and I was one of the lucky ones. She made it look like I died and turned me into her minion. Kept me compliant by threatening Ana, here, and Julio. I've been, uh, keeping tabs on them." This brought Ana's glare lasered in on him. "And we just found out tonight her fiancé was an Agent."

"Bullshit." Wasn't Bennett going to believe anything?

"Duuude, that's fucked up." Thanks, Mercury.

"Whaaaat?" Kaitlyn looked like she wanted to hear more.

E didn't know her well. She was relatively new, but she was an excellent fighter. He'd been glad he didn't have to face her in hand-to-hand. Rumor had it, she rarely transitioned into her wolf, but no one at Sigma knew why.

E gave a little shrug, hands still raised. "Madame G wants her and the boy, so Agent G was ordered to bring both of them in. I think…" He scanned their surroundings. The compound was probably the most secure place where he could speak freely, but still, they were out in the open. "I think she suspects me of not being her good little pet. Now can we talk inside?"

Commander Fitzsimmons jutted his chin in Ana's direction. "What's your last name?"

"Esposito." E was proud of her, her voice didn't shake.

"Ah," Kaitlyn nodded. "Agent *E*. I get it."

"How do you spell your first name, Ana?" Why would Mercury be asking that?

A tense silence filled the next few moments before the commander hit him with a few more questions. Riding the edge of patience, and hating to keep his wife and kid in the open, E gritted his teeth and answered the questions the commander threw out. "Julio Esposito. It happened over ten years ago. Ask Ana if you want the exact date, my memory about the specifics got a little hazy from the smoke inhalation and blood-letting."

"She says it all concurs." E frowned at Mercury before realizing the shifter's mate, Dani, must be behind the questions, sending them mentally to her mate who then passed the info on.

He wouldn't mind seeing Dani again. She used to train with him and X, while seeking vengeance for her family that was slaughtered by feral shifters. Since she was a good kid, she quickly realized her error thinking that joining Sigma was the right path to take in life. And with Sigma's only retirement plan being death, well, that left her a little stuck. Until Madame G decided to use her as an incubator to grow Mercury's baby so she could corrupt the little life.

But the tenacious young lady found a way out, and with a little prodding from X, ran to the Guardians, found Mercury, fell in love with him, and as far as E knew, found a way to remove the madam's taint from their bouncing bundle of joy.

He and X had made themselves scarce hunting rogue shifters that were Sigma spies when the baby cleansing news broke, but they had witnessed some of the fallout. Sigma recruits were still patching up damage in the wing that Madame G left behind when she felt the severing of her bond with the baby.

Ha! Good.

"Put all your weapons on the ground, then spread 'em, hands against the wall. Ana and Julio, stay where you're at. Kaitlyn, search Ana and the boy first, and then Agent E." Commander Fitzsimmons fired off the orders and waited for E's obedience.

The staid leader of the West Creek Guardians had garnered some serious respect, and with his order, earned a little more from E, letting Kaitlyn do the pat down. Though Mercury and Bennett were mated shifters, it'd still kill E to stand weaponless while they patted his wife and son down. Somehow, having a female do it, even given she had the mad skills to kill them all, made him feel better and would put his family at ease.

As much as he despised going weaponless, he had to get Ana and Julio secured. Flipping a few buckles and unsnapping a few buttons, E shrugged out of the set-up that wrapped around his shoulders and waist. He gestured at Ana to take her gear, or rather his old gear, off. Then it was the tedious task of unearthing all the knives and small pistols he had stashed around his six-foot-two frame. Out of the corner of his eye, he could see Ana's horrified expression at the growing pile of metal, including silver, and Julio's eyes wide as saucers, his mouth forming a "whoa."

"There. Done." He turned to face the lodge and put his hands on the cool logs next to the doorframe.

"Hold still. Anyone moves before I'm done, Mercury's putting a cap in your ass." Kaitlyn's long legs covered the ground quickly to stand next to them. "Except for you, kid. You're cute."

She shot Julio a quick smile and he returned it shyly. Her tone was light as she frisked his boy, always telling him what to expect. She repeated the process with Ana, who looked as uncomfortable as the day she had met his dad so many years ago. But she had visibly relaxed by the time the amicable redhead was done.

"You two play the freeze game while I pat down the big guy here."

With more brusqueness, and hell of a lot more force, Kaitlyn frisked him. E's balls still throbbed at her curt efficiency checking all of his nooks and crannies for hidden metal.

"He's clean," she announced, before opening the door to the lodge, adding a "surprisingly" under her breath.

"Mercury, Kaitlyn, take Ana and Julio to room two." The commander shuffled in behind E, along with Mercury and Bennett. "Agent E, you're coming with me and Bennett."

E rounded on the commander. "I stay with them." Mercury and Bennett's armed hands didn't raise, didn't twitch, but both males got very still, a predatory gleam in their eye.

Commander Fitzsimmons spoke low, maybe Ana could hear from where she came to a stop to watch E's reaction, maybe her human ears were too weak. "Think about it, Agent. You can't walk in here expecting to be treated like an honored guest. We all have scars from fighting you, and your silver switchblade and silver-laced bullets. If what you say is true, and you brought them here because you trust us to protect them, then let us do that." His voice dropped even lower. "Even if we have to protect them from you."

E's jaw nearly cracked from the pressure of clenched teeth. He wanted to smash the ruddy bastard's face in, pound him into the concrete. But…the commander was right. The threat to his wife and son was Sigma, and it was because of him.

Meeting Ana's unwavering gaze, he gave a sharp nod that she echoed back.

*****

A satisfied grunt told X she was close. Sliding back up the male's rigid length, raking her nails down his muscled-ripped chest, she undulated her hips at the top before sliding back down, letting the male's girth fill her while she clutched the back of the chair for leverage.

Agent J thrust his hips up to prompt her into a faster pace. Running her finger under his jaw, she brought his attention off her breasts. His eyes were glazed with heat, desperately urging her to ride him faster, speed him to the finish.

When she had gotten back to the compound after her partner dropped her off on the side of the road, X knew she had to get down to business and find out what the plans were for Ana and Julio. There was only a small window of opportunity. No news had spread about a kid arriving and E wasn't back yet. Just sent her a "FUBAR" text. Things had gone the fucked-up route for them before, but the "beyond all relief" part meant E had defected, had chosen his family over the madam's destruction. Chatter hadn't started yet about how an Agent went rogue over some civilians. Therefore, everyone, including Madame G, would see X hanging out, getting her freak on with another Agent, and that'd be her, "I don't know anything" alibi when E's deception was discovered.

Agent J nuzzled her neck, licking and nipping. If he struck too soon, she'd rip his head back and ask questions, but it'd be harder to alter his thoughts of what had transpired between them. It was better to inquire pre-bite, convince them there'd been no conversation, and then let the biting happen, to further gloss over that little memory. There'd been some trial and error, but X had finally found a sweet spot for her little hypnosis talent. Sex didn't always have to be involved, but in this case, she needed information and the vampire would die horribly before giving it to her otherwise.

X picked the Agent because unlike her usual informant, Demetrius, the vampire didn't deviate from Sigma's goals, carrying them out with cool efficiency. Need an innocent shifter tortured until you can no longer recognize him? Call Agent J. New inauspicious female to "train?" Agent J was first in line. If Madame G wanted a kid tortured, he'd do it.

Aaaand that's exactly why X was in flagrante with him at the moment. Long ago, she'd culminated a flirtatious relationship with the male, which occasionally went further than just dirty talk. He was a virile, deadly vampire, like catnip for the female Agents and recruits, and just the kind of source X could tap into when needed.

Leaning in to lick the rim of his ear, X decided now was the time, soon he'd dominate her body.

Sitting back, she caught his cardinal hued eyes and concentrated hard, feeling him go still inside of her.

"Tell me, J," she purred, "what's your next project?"

His vacant gaze wavered for a moment, and she worried she'd gotten him too caught up in lust to focus. "Agent E's brat. Get him started transitioning now since the boss thinks his daddy was such a success."

The disdain in the last statement was resounding. Whereas X could get away with being less malicious and depraved because of her looks and gender, Agent E was viewed with contempt.

Not only because he could refuse certain duties, but because he could, and did, get away with it. X and her partner were too valuable to Madame G for just that reason. They weren't mindless killers. While that irked their mistress, it garnered her respect and she entrusted them with the more delicate missions. It made them targets of distain for other, less-discerning Agents.

"Oh?" X squeezed her inner muscles around him, and Agent J gazed more intently at her. "And how exactly will she do that?"

Little was known about how Agents are actually enhanced. It involved a lot of injections, and while Agents proliferated readily, there wasn't a high survival rate. Madame G had turned quite a few of her recruits, even ones who were clearly too weak to survive, mostly to study them for what traits made for more viable transitions.

Agent J tried rocking his hips, but X concentrated harder until he stilled. "She'll start the injections tailored to his body weight, using the same formula she used for dear daddy."

"What's the formula?"

Sweat broke out on his brow. "A mixture of vampire and shifter serum that she says some incantation over as she adds her own blood."

Interesting. "And what about the kid's mother?"

"Collateral." His body shuddered, wanting to seek its release. X didn't have much time. "She'll enhance her but without the blood bond, so she'll become strong enough to sustain what the madam plans for her. If E interferes with the kid, he risks *her* and has to live with the guilt of what happens to her."

X didn't even have to ask what would happen to Ana. The insane vampires the madam employed liked new blood and new bodies. And if she wanted Ana to suffer greatly, well, the vampire prisoners Madame G's torture and experiments made insane needed blood. When they were done, there wasn't usually much of a body left. Madame G probably wouldn't even wait for E to interfere, but throw Ana to the fangers anyway because he pissed her off.

"Where will she keep them?"

"Both will be in the lower levels, but the kid will be in the east wing, one level further down, kept far from his parents."

Figures. That'd make escape and/or rescue extremely challenging.

Undulating her hips, making him let out a shock of air, X centered herself, letting her will flow through her voice. "I asked you nothing. We didn't talk. I wanted to get back at E for dumping me on the side of the road."

Mindlessly, Agent J nodded. Releasing his stare, she shoved his face into her neck. He struck hard with his fangs, pulling blood as they both rode the wave of pleasure to their finish. It wasn't passionate, just genetic. Vampire bites finished the job penetration started, so X's release was physical only. She'd become quite adept at shutting her mind off to what her body was cursed with drawing out.

The vampire's head lolled back, spent, drunk off her shifter blood, and disoriented from her subtle, but efficacious hypnosis. X straightened, letting his shaft slide out and fall against his belly. Reaching for her clothes, she dressed with methodical precision and left.

Chapter Seven

E was settled into a nice, cozy cell that even had windows. They were high and placed at strategic angles. They'd be hell on a vampire prisoner, but since he was only somewhat vampire, high noon didn't bother him. Well, not much. A pair of sunglasses would be nice when the sun rose next.

Not bothering to sit, E faced the barred door and crossed his arms over his chest, which felt absolutely naked without his weapons. His jaw continued to throb, not quite healed from the right hook Bennett had given him before he'd entered the cell.

"That's for shooting Sarah," Bennett had growled.

And yeah, E had put a bullet in her shoulder. Her *shoulder*, not her heart. "Please, it only wounded her." E had shot back, spitting out blood, not mentioning it had helped them fake her death, and got X and E off the hook when they were sent to bring in X's niece.

Commander Fitzsimmons dismissed Bennett once E was settled. Then faced him from the other side of the cell door. "Lay it all out. What are you and X up to?"

The male cut straight to the heart. E drew in a long cleansing breath. "I would love to Commander, but it will do X no good if I sit here and spill her business. My first priority is, and always has been, my family. My second is my partner, and whatever she's up to is her business."

Commander Fitzsimmons leveled a look at E, who gazed back unflinchingly. "Say she had something to hide," his eyes narrowed, "would you know what it is?"

Soooo…Shit. Did this mean the Guardian leader knew X's secret, knew she had a secret but didn't know what it was, or just suspected the Agent wasn't an open book to Madame G?

"She's closer to me than a sibling." E chose his words carefully, "So yeah, say she was hiding something, I would know what it is."

He felt a negative emotion building from the other male. Rage. If E's senses were correct, the commander was getting angry, and it didn't take E long to deduce why.

"We're close, Commander, but not *close*." Even saying that was endangering his partner. If it got out that E and X weren't getting busy between the sheets, it'd give Madame G a major reason to rein them in and interrogate their insides out of them.

A muscle ticked on the inside of the male's jaw as rage was replaced by regard.

"You want to know why? How can that be possible when she carries my stank?" E could give the Guardian this, for helping his family. "She's sexy as hell and maybe things would've been different. The madam was still trying to break her mentally, which meant a lot of physical…training." Their goes the rage spiking again. "I'd just come out of transition to whatever you'd call me now, hormones raging, plowing through whoever they threw at me. Until her." E shook his head. "She reminded me of everything I lost and got it through my foggy, ravaged brain everything I still had to lose. I can honestly tell you, Commander, that without her, I don't know how I would've survived once some semblance of my right mind came back to me. Without a doubt, I can tell you, I would've messed up along the way, and Ana and my son would've paid for it."

"Where is X now?"

The poor bastard. E wished he could protect the stolid, honorable male from his next statement. "At the compound, doing her job." Wait for it… "Trading for information about why there's an order out for Ana and Julio."

Commander Fitzsimmons remained still like a statue, hazel eyes boring into E's. Finally, he gave a curt nod and made to turn away.

"It doesn't mean anything," E said gruffly, knowing exactly how the male felt. "It's a business exchange. Doing business like we were taught. If we aren't debasing ourselves on a constant basis, the boss starts thinking we've gone good. She wants us to be mindless, rutting beasts, following her every command." The commander wasn't staring into the cell anymore, but was turned away, head partially lowered, glaring at the floor. "At least she's reached a station where she can have some say in her transactions. It wasn't always that way."

Agent X was good at her job, and she excelled at using her body to gather the information she and E needed. Each time, E had advised against it and told her they'd find another way. But every other way was too risky and might lead Madame G to question their actions, question their commitments to Sigma. It would lead to their restriction, or worse, torture, and, even worse still, retraining. Because E and X were too valuable, too highly skilled, for Madame G to ever give them up.

When the commander's gaze flicked back, E was staggered by the emotion visible. Grief. The male was hurting, but accepted the situation. E knew his pain. Every night he stood outside of Ana's house, peeking between the curtains, watching that bastard Griffin, caress her, kiss her full lips, pull her lush body into his, E had the same pain reflecting in his eyes. It was the agony of witnessing the one you were meant to be with, your mate, giving herself to another.

*****

"You're…So you are…" Ana drifted off and the tall Guardian sitting across the table from her flashed her a little smile.

~75~

"Do I turn furry and howl? Yes." The tall, beautiful, copper-haired female replied.

Ana gave a gusty exhale, peering down to Julio, sitting to her right. He appeared much more thrilled than she was, but Ana's mind had a hard time accepting the facts. Really, until she saw firsthand someone changing forms or drinking blood with fangs, she couldn't buy the vampire/werewolf story. Her mind wanted to substitute perfectly absurd, yet more valid, reasons for how Griffin acted, and why her late husband cut off heads and burned bodies. Secret agency and government testing? Sure. She was shot up with a drug and was hallucinating? Absolutely. Her dead husband, who was really kidnapped by vampires, taking her to wolf-shifters to keep safe. Nope. Not possible.

"I could prove it to you, but we have to undress, and we don't change back with clothes on, so..." Kaitlyn drifted on, mirth hidden in her words.

"I'll pass on the offer, but thank you. So what now?"

Kaitlyn gestured to the large one-way mirror behind her. "We have someone back there to record you. Why don't you start at the beginning?"

Ana was stuck. Where was the beginning? She thought she had a perfectly normal life until three days ago when her son was attacked.

Seeing her difficulty, Kaitlyn gave her another reassuring smile and Ana was immensely glad they had left her in the room and not one of the other large, imposing males. Especially the one with the unique coloring she heard called Mercury. His name was quite fitting with silver gleaming through his black hair and dark eyes, eyes that were disconcerting in how they seemed to not miss one single detail.

"Go back as far as when Agent E was still your husband. How was your marriage? Was there anything weird that you noticed before they told you he had died? Anything you thought was odd or didn't think of as abnormal until you look back on it." Kaitlyn leaned forward across the table, and folded her hands, a comforting presence.

Ana sat back and thought for a moment. "We were happy. Young, broke, and happy Julio." She almost corrected herself to call him Agent E, but no, she was talking about her husband, the love of her life, and whomever he was now didn't change that. "He loved his job. He'd wanted to be a police officer since he was a boy. His dad was a cop and his mom died of breast cancer before he was five, so it was just him and his dad. I lived with my Nana since my parents had been just kids when they had me. They got in with a bad crowd, and I lost both of them before I even knew them." Ana fiddled with her hands, wondering how far in depth she should go. "We met when I was a junior and my high school toured the college where he was a freshman. We got married as soon as he finished the police academy and I graduated high school and got a job.

Then I went to college and we lived in a tiny apartment. We were happy."

Sadness as to what could have been threatened to swamp Ana. It wasn't a foreign emotion by far, so she reached over to run her hands over little Julio's hair. So much like his father's—tightly curled, cut short to the scalp, just like his dad had always worn it, still wore it. Man, would she ever get used to thinking that way? That the husband she'd mourned deeply for over a decade was still alive?

Ana told Kaitlyn about *that* night, not worrying that Julio was in the room; he'd heard it all before. She described the joy of the pregnancy news, and the devastation of the days after, to the numbness of the following weeks. Even now, not a thing stood out to Ana as unusual.

"When did you start dating again?"

"Gosh, like five years after Julio passed, or didn't pass, whatever."

"Were you looking to date, or did men start approaching you?"

Could there have been more Agents than Griffin trying to get to her and her son? That was…that was just…really insulting, and frightening. Frowning, she ran through the men she had dated in her head.

"I've never approached anyone. I wasn't looking for a relationship, but I wasn't opposed to it. I was lonely." Ana gave her best rundown of the men she'd had in her life. There were two sort of serious ones before Griffin and a handful of ones she'd just dated and cut things off with before anything serious started. "Griffin pursued me more than the others. He was thoughtful, considerate, professionally successful…or so I thought." Scorn poured out of her voice. Professionally successful was right, his job was to con her into marrying him.

Kaitlyn glanced toward Julio. "Hey bucko, any of the dudes give you weirdo vibes?"

Julio lifted one shoulder. "They were okay. I didn't like Griffin because he made Mom put all the pictures of her and Dad away."

"He didn't make me, we just agreed it was appropriate." Ana let her defenses drop. She knew it had bothered Julio, but had no idea the depth of hurt he felt. She hadn't seen it through a ten-year-old boy's eyes who never got to know his dad, but undoubtedly idolized him.

"What brought you to our doorstep?" Kaitlyn read into the silence between Ana and Julio and moved them past the tension.

"Go ahead," Ana encouraged the sullen boy, "tell her about the other night."

As Julio told his story, Kaitlyn peppered him with questions about the kid who claimed to have the coveted Pokémon card. Then Ana described a censored version of how Griffin changed after the incident with Julio, and then the events of the day. Or the previous day. How late was it?

Once she drifted off, Kaitlyn hesitated for a few moments. "All righty then, let's get you two set up for the night. One of us will guard you twenty-four/seven, so don't be alarmed if you see a big dude hanging around outside your door. I'm taking first shift, though." She stood up, moving gracefully to the door. As it swung open, she faced them. "After you."

*****

X was distinctly aware that there was no comforting presence wrapping her in his heat, in his protection, like he always did during her dreams. He was there, otherwise she would be awake, wracked by the nightmares that had plagued her for twelve years. She let her awareness spread and found him sitting with his back to her on the edge of her dream bed, in her dream room, which was identical to her dorm in the Sigma compound except for the blurred edges.

This was the first time she actually saw him in her dream, but like in the first dream appearance, she knew it was him. He was always a comforting presence, holding her. She never acknowledged he was there and kept the stolen moments to herself. It was the only thing that was hers alone.

Exhaling softly, X didn't bother to ask what was wrong. Of course she knew; there was so much. She was supremely grateful she had showered before she crawled into bed. No need to showcase her exploits, insulting the male who protected her dreams, never speaking to her, never asking to do anything more than allow him to hold her and keep the nightmares at bay.

"I understand," he finally said, as if acknowledging her thoughts.

"It doesn't matter," she countered.

"It does." He twisted around, perceptive hazel eyes drifting up her body that was encased in only a T-shirt, underwear, and no less than two knives. "You do what you need to do, Alexandria." Her blood ran cold; he knew exactly who she was. It'd been so long since anyone had called her that; it felt like an insult to the girl she once was. "We'll help you destroy Madame G, get you out, and then we can deal with us."

"I'm afraid there is only a one-way ticket for me at the end of all this, Rhys." Sadness and regret laced her voice.

"Dani made it out," the Guardian commander pointed out.

"And Madame G's still alive. She needs to die. She needs to be destroyed. She needs to be sent somewhere to suffer for eternity." Damn, that felt good to say out loud, even if it was only in a dream world. Not even she and E talked out loud about their plans, it was just understood. It was also understood that if one word was uttered and heard, they'd die. "And I don't know why she's so powerful, or what we're up against when we do go against her. If the time ever comes, I will get only one shot to destroy her."

Rhys turned so he was sitting more fully on the bed, leaning over her, and she indulged herself, her eyes drifting over his features. Over the years, they'd only fought each other, where she had admired his form, his style, his ruggedly-handsome physique. She knew that the brown of his eyes were interspersed with the brightest green, were sharply intelligent, and now they were warmed with concern and tenderness for her.

"I had to be with someone else today." She blurted it out and cursed herself at ruining a good moment. Didn't matter. She shouldn't get good moments, they were dangerous.

His expression hardened for less than a second before softening toward her again, this time with anguish shining bright. "I know," he said quietly. "As much as I wish you had enough vampire in you to render you impotent because I'm your true mate, it would've gotten you killed long ago."

She was stunned and dismayed at his declaration. "You need to move on Rhys. There is no 'us.' Next time we meet, I will no doubt put a bullet or blade in you, like I always do. You need to still be able to do the same to me."

For so long, he thought her the enemy, not intending to kill her, only stop her. But while she could make sure not to hit anything vital, she had to be ruthless, with him and all the Guardians. They all sported scars from her silver hardware. She was the same, and call her a masochist, but she was insanely proud of the marks made by Rhys. "Find a nice little shifter female to move on with. Or a ton of human women."

She expected his face to cloud over, get angry, something other than afflicted. "You are mine." He leaned down close, his firm dream lips inches above her own. "I haven't been with anyone in years. At first, I would in retaliation for smelling you on another male. Then I couldn't. I don't want to. I will wait for you."

Tears threatened to well up and, no. Just no. "There's nothing to wait for."

"We'll see." He was leaning down closer, ever so slowly his lips closing in on hers, like he couldn't help himself. She intended to ignore her pounding heart, argue that he couldn't wait for her, she wasn't worth it.

Agent X, report to my suite!

Instantly, the dream world disappeared to be replaced by a sharper image of her room as X's eyes flew open. Madame G sounded pissed, filling her with dread. Her malignant leader rarely showed emotion, keeping watch over her people like a bird of prey. X shook off the dream, donned her clothing and gear, and prepared to become well-acquainted with pain.

Chapter Eight

"I wondered if you'd venture down here." E was stretched out on his bunk, hands behind his head, legs crossed at the ankles, staring up at the bare ceiling.

He didn't bother to look at his visitor, wasn't sure what the reception would be. Dani Santini stood on the other side of the bars. E could sense her mate, Mercury, at the end of the corridor. The last time he saw her, E was trying to capture her to bring her back to the compound.

"I had to say thank you while I had the chance."

Well, that's…unexpected. "For what?" he grunted.

Dani crossed her arms over her chest, pinning him with eyes the color of rich coffee. "For training me not to be a sadistic killer and for only half-assing your attempt to catch me that night in the woods. Oh yes, and for killing Mason before he killed me."

E sat up, swinging his legs down to the floor and resting his elbows on his knees. Finally, he turned to look at her, sweeping his eyes over her athletic body from head to toe. She looked good.

When he first met her, she seemed like a naïve kid in a big, bad world. Then he watched her grow into a capable fighter, but she had always held a hint of innocence, a bit of insecurity about her role in the organization. Now, she stood with confidence, facing him unflinchingly. "Don't glorify me, Dani. I'm not a good person."

She had the audacity to roll her eyes. "I agree. You're kind of a dick. I'm still saying thank you, whether it puts a hole in your man card or not."

Smirking because he couldn't help himself, he stood and took the two steps across his tiny cell to stand across from her in the doorway. "Watching you get away, then somehow manage to get Madame G's taint off you and your baby, better than any Super Bowl party I'd ever been to as a human. It was epic."

The supernatural tantrum Madame G had thrown was astronomic. When he was clear of flying debris, he'd wallowed in it. For the first time in what was left of his life, he felt like maybe he was on the right track, finally being rewarded with a victory scored over the madam's influence.

He turned his attention back to Dani. "How's the baby?"

Would she tell him? Or would he be treated like an evil Sigma Agent again? If she didn't discuss her child with him, he'd understand. But it'd feel like shit, man, it really would.

A smile lit up her face. "He's pretty epic himself. Big, he's a big little guy."

The kid must be what, like nine months old or something? It made E sick every time he thought about how it could've gone if Dani hadn't gotten away, if Mercury hadn't escaped, if their baby had stayed tied to Sigma. Sickening.

"What'd you name him?" Was this really a conversation he was having? Talking kids with an old friend? Those scenarios weren't meant for his life anymore. Less than twenty-four hours being away from Sigma and he was already being pelted with moments of normalcy.

"Dante." Dani's voice radiated the natural pride of a mother.

"Cool." E nodded. "That's very cool."

The convo drifted off into awkward silence. He didn't dare ask further about Dante—anything could and would be used against him and others in the court of Madame G—and Dani was smart enough not to elaborate.

"We'll help Ana and Julio, E."

Not a shocker. They were two innocent people targeted by Sigma, of course the Guardians would help them. He waited for the rest.

"But here's the thing. Madame G is going to strike hard and fast once she learns we have those two *and* you. We're building our numbers within the pack, but we can't ignore threats to our people and utilize too many of our resources to protect your family. Commander Fitzsimmons figures she'll plan her attacks so that we have to spread our numbers thin, leaving the lodge more vulnerable."

Fuck. He didn't think beyond getting his wife and kid here. Proof E's intelligence took a backseat to his feelings for his family, and why those feelings were dangerous. *Here* meant safety, and it didn't occur to him they wouldn't not be safe. The Guardians used the ancient protections of their people to mask their location, along with state-of-the-art technology to monitor the surrounding woods and enhance building security. But if there was no one here to guard them...

"Then what?"

"The commander will talk to you more, but I told him I wanted to come see you before the shit hit the fan. Anyway, he said you might have to go on the run with them."

Not a good option. "She can find me anywhere if she needs to." Madame G bound herself by blood to all of her Agents. It was like a homing beacon, a big reason why no one could escape.

"Welll..." Dani sounded like he wasn't going to like her idea. "We have a theory that might be worth a shot."

"I'm listening."

"When I mated Mercury, it was like our bond overrode Madame G's, and my body and Dante's were purged."

So that's how they did it. Man, if that ever got out, there'd be some repentant Agents trying to find them some shifters to mate with. "I don't mean to state the obvious, but I'm not a shifter."

"Duh. Give us some of your blood, and our research guy," *They have a research guy? Oh right, that older shifter Dani's mate busted out last year.* "will see if he can find out anything. But," she shrugged, "it's something. We know she uses vampire blood to enhance her people, and vampires have their own bonding practices."

"Except she's a vamp herself. Will a kind-of vampire mating a non-vampire out bond a maniacal vampire's bond?" That's if…if, Ana would number one, agree to it, and two, follow through when the whole drinking blood bit came up.

"Dunno. Think about it. Have any vampire Agents ever mated, that you know of?"

"Maybe in other Sigma chapters."

Dani shook her head. "Doubt it. None are as comprehensive as Freemont's chapter, and from what we know, only Madame G experiments on her Agents."

"So then, will I die? Ten years of her infesting me, I'm not human anymore." He hadn't felt human since he went down in the warehouse fire.

"There's always a chance, but Doc Garreth thinks her conversion process digs into your DNA to alter genes. We think that while her scientists came up with a way to insert vampire traits, Madame G's blood alone couldn't do that. So the change might be all you."

His enhancements were there to stay. Fucking fabulous. To be real, he didn't want to lose his abilities, not at this critical time. He needed them to stay at the top of the Agent game and figure out how to kill Madame G.

"I don't know that Ana'll ever agree to it," he finally admitted. "To her, her husband died over ten years ago. I'm just someone she probably regrets finding out ever existed because I remind her of everything that was lost."

Dani's eyes held somber acceptance for him, a shade short of pity. She knew how it was for Agents. She was almost one herself, though she'd been spared the dirty details since Madame G had other plans for her. "Don't underestimate what a mother will do for her son."

*****

"We need to what?" Ana's voice could cut steel.

"Our Guardian numbers at the lodge are dwindling." Commander Fitzsimmons remained unfazed by her disbelief. No scratch that, her utter inability to accept the crazy shit he was spewing. "We have Guardians fanning out to protect the local colonies whose clans are getting hit hard by attacks from recruits and Agents. Soon, she'll attack here, and she has the numbers to eventually find this place and make it inside. They have before, but we don't have the level of protection we normally do. Especially not to protect children."

Children? The plural word sunk in and damn, there was more than just Julio at risk. But mate the

Agent who used to be her husband? Mate, not marry. It was crazy. She feared a blood exchange with the man who resembled a tougher, more virile version of her already masculine, vigorous late husband.

Not only that, the commander had added, they also needed to consummate the bond. She found out she had been sleeping with the enemy only two days ago, a man who had been sent to monitor her, had tried to kill her son, and then kidnap both of them. She was trying to dump that baggage and now a man who supposedly changes into a wolf was telling her that she needed to swap blood with her no-longer-dead husband and have sex with him? To save her and her son?

"Once it's done," the nonplussed commander continued, "we can arm you and give Agent E his weapons back, make you some maps to the woods, and send Kaitlyn with you to go into hiding."

"Kaitlyn doesn't have a mate or children?"

Commander Fitzsimmons grimly shook his head.

"Does that mean there's a good chance we might end up killed or captured?"

"It's a possibility." He leveled his intense hazel eyes on her. "We'll deal with that if need be. But your son is comfortable with her, and she's an excellent Guardian." A brief hesitation. "One without quite the history with Agent E that the rest of us have."

"Some bad blood, huh?"

He considered his words. "Perhaps they might not be as open-minded as Kaitlyn would be."

"Gotcha." Ana looked up from her twisting hands. They were sitting in the corner of the rec room, Julio playing Xbox with a pale-haired young teen boy, having the time of his life. She'd never let him play as many video games in his ten years as he had the last two days they'd been staying at the lodge. "Commander, you all have been absolutely honest."

Brutally so. She'd asked Kaitlyn what being an Agent entailed. Even Ana could tell the female had first mentally consulted her boss, and then shrewdly gauged the authenticity of Ana's reaction to the details. One of the many ways they had determined her and Julio's lack of culpability in the whole Sigma scheme. After helping them get settled, Kaitlyn had pulled Ana aside, stripped down, and shifted into a wolf. Ana had damn near pissed herself, but any disbelief had gone out of the window. Julio, then came out to the hallway and asked to pet the giant red wolf before Kaitlyn went back to her own cabin to shift back.

Sigh…What a world she'd been thrown into. "That man, Agent E, how much of my husband is left? And if this bonding thing works, then what? Is he something, someone, I want to be attached to for the rest of my life?"

The silence that followed didn't bode well for the answer. Commander Fitzsimmons' eyes never wavered from hers as he internally ruminated over what to say.

"Your husband's human innocence is gone." His voice was barely audible to her human ears. "Is there anything left of him? Yes, or you wouldn't be here. He is most definitely changed. In a good way or a bad way? It was intended for evil, but is he evil? I don't think so. You will have to make your own decision. If I had a mate," he paused, clearing his throat, "and she was captured by Sigma, but eventually her actions suggested she wasn't fully adopted into their indoctrination, and maybe even working undetectably against Sigma, then I would understand the position she was put in. I wouldn't give up on her."

His words tore at her. "Even with what they would've done during their time as an Agent? Could you be mated to an Agent after that?" she whispered.

Those perceptive hazel eyes never strayed as he thought his answer over. "That is something you'll have to reconcile within yourself. What's done is done. What an Agent might still have to do…" A shadow flitted across his face. "I guess, the reasons behind their actions are what makes the difference."

There was a story there. She suddenly felt a kinship with the stranger in front of her. This man recently had to make his own reconciliation about someone and it strained him greatly.

"If Agent E agrees, I'll do it. For my son's safety."

*****

What a relief, I don't have to drink blood. Ana sat in the original interrogation room where she had been brought when they first arrived. Agent E sat stiffly next to her, while Julio was down in the rec room playing video games.

They had both been summoned to meet with the commander to discuss their upcoming nuptials, or mating, or whatever it was called by non-human species. Ana found out that the Guardian's doctor wasn't an MD doctor, but a PhD researcher who had spent years working and secretly learning medicine in human hospitals. The doctor, Garreth, had studied E's blood and confirmed both vampire and shifter elements. He deduced that since the serum given to alter Agents contained elements from both species, either form of mating may be successful. Or not. Since Ana wasn't sure how she was going to stomach a mouthful of fresh blood without vomiting it right back up, she opted for a shifter mating. That is, after she had asked the good doctor if there were blood-borne diseases she could catch from Agent E. Garreth had explained that those kinds of diseases didn't cross the human threshold.

One less thing to worry about.

"We'll mate you like we would a shifter pair, using a special dagger to meld your blood." Commander Fitzsimmons eyed them both, waiting for objections. Ana just felt numb. "I can do the ceremony, unless either of you have an issue with that."

Ana weakly shook her head while E answered with a gruff, "You're fine."

"Ana, you need to call your work. Tell them the wedding's off, you need a change, and you and Julio are moving. Say sorry for the short notice, but after all you've been through, it was just too much. Something along those lines."

Awesome. She'd be the dick who just up and quit work. Over a guy. But it sounded plausible, and they all knew her history.

"Jace will take care of cleaning and selling the house, wrap up all the loose ends." The commander studied the two of them, sitting side by side, reading their rigid, uncomfortable body language. "Would you two like some time in here to talk before the ceremony?"

"Yeah, that'd be great," E muttered.

"Sure," Ana mumbled.

Commander Fitzsimmons rose to his imposing height. "The recorders are off. Dani will be in her office so just knock when you're ready to head back to your rooms. She'll hear you and call me."

After he left and the door swung closed, Ana continued to study the table, while E sat with his arms crossed, staring at the wall.

"I'm sorry," E said abruptly.

Ana's brows drew together. "For what?"

"All of this. And that you have to mate me even though you've moved on."

Ana didn't need special hearing to detect the faint edge of bitterness in his last statement, and her anger was quick to flare. "What was I supposed to do? Going through life alone is not a lot of fun. Going through life alone after having lost my best friend and husband?" She shook her head. "I was miserable. I mean, Julio and I were happy, but after Nana died it was just me and him. He lost his first tooth, and who was there to join in the celebration? He learned to ride a bike, and who could I call and tell? Yeah, the hard times were bad enough. The good times were almost worse, because then I could see how alone I really was."

E's brow creased, like he'd never thought of what it was like to share in all of life's pleasures and disappointments with no one. Not. A. Soul.

"There was no one, Julio. Agent E. Whatever."

"E is fine," he answered gravely, studying his hands.

"So, yeah, I moved on. I dated and was ready to marry again. It was nice to feel cared for, to have adult company, have a shoulder to lean on. I find myself grateful that even though Griffin was conning me, he put on a good show."

"I'm sorry," E repeated, his voice heavy with emotion.

Those two words pissed Ana off.

"Maybe you should be." She nearly shouted at him. "It's not like I could fall in love with anyone else after you." His startled expression lifted to meet her incensed one. "It's not like any of this hell was our fault. So you know what you can do? Mate me and try not to get killed for real. Because the only blessing I felt like I had was not having to tell a son he lost his father, since he never knew you anyway." Ana stood up to stomp toward the door. "But now he knows you, however briefly. So don't die."

Chapter Nine

"I want you to tell me everything, you know, before we…" Ana drifted off. She was in a little cabin that had been vacant since this pack of Guardians took up residence in West Creek. It had been tidied and freshened for their overnight stay. There they sat, side by side, on the already made bed. Ana in a simple ivory dress, E wearing borrowed slacks and a dress shirt, under Mercury's strict orders to, "Take them off before you two do it."

The commander had mated them privately, not even Julio was present. She hadn't wanted to get the boy's hopes up, like his parents were getting remarried or something. Right now this mating was for survival.

Steeling her resolve, she continued. "I want to know everything you've done, no barriers, no more secrets. We start this new relationship completely open. You know what my life has been like, what I do for a living, who I've been with, so it's your turn."

"Ana." E's eyes filled with trepidation. "You don't know what you're asking. It's awful and it's done. I can't take back any of it."

Sighing, Ana stared straight ahead. "We haven't been able to talk, to catch up. You're a stranger, but you're not. You say my husband died that night, but when I look at you, I'm seeing him. It's hard to separate the two, you need to understand that."

Turning toward him, waiting until his dark-brown eyes met hers, she pressed on. "You say you're not Julio Esposito, but part of this Agent E," she gestured up and down his body, "is him. If it makes you feel better, I'm not Ana Esposito anymore. I'm Ana Esposito, widow and single mom. It's been my identity since that night. I've had other relationships, a whole life, other than the one you and I had together."

Her dead husband, wait, new husband. No, that wasn't right, either. She had to quit thinking of him as her dead husband. Or husband at all. Mate. Her mate took a deep breath and started talking. He began with the sexcapades from when he woke up changed, and how he met his partner, Agent X.

"Trust me, when it comes to X, I can't tell you for your own safety. And hers. Just know, we're close and she's extremely important to me."

"You really care for her?"

He paused. "Yes. It benefitted both of us greatly and offered us each some protection to let others think we had a certain type of relationship. But I didn't have to pretend to care for her."

Agent X definitely intrigued her.

He continued on with the more stomach-churning details of his duty with Sigma: the people he hurt, who he killed, who he seduced and then sometimes killed, and why. It made her sick, that his mind and body would be used as a weapon when he'd been nothing but tender, loving, and protective when he was hers, when he was human. He ended with how he hid his activity, watching her and Julio, paying off prostitutes to say he was with them all night, not just for the half hour it took to get covered in their scent.

She knew he was done when he trailed off, head down, hands folded on his lap, awaiting her judgment. Her heart hurt. He was so strong and so damaged, so ashamed yet so repentant, so determined but so lost. Maybe their mating started as nothing but survival, but right now it felt like so much more.

"Twice now you've given up everything for me. We've been given another chance and neither of us knows for how long. But one thing we do know, is that we're finally a family again." She gave a weak, wry smile. "Albeit an untraditional one."

His expression stole her breath with its intensity. "You're phenomenal."

Faster than she could see him move, he flipped her back on the bed, his powerful body covering hers, his lips crushing hers, swallowing her gasp. Ana managed to wiggle her hands free to cup his face in awe. She had her husband with her again.

How many times had she prayed for this, knowing the futileness of her efforts? How often had she dreamed of his touch, of his scent enveloping her, only to wake and find an empty bed, or worse, one of the men she'd been in a relationship with? The brief flare of hope at finding a man next to her, only to realize it wasn't the one she'd been dreaming about.

He was here now. It wasn't a miracle, but a devastating tragedy, a transforming work of evil that took him away. Despite it all, he was back. She met his energy with equal verve of her own, relishing his lips and his length pressing against her belly.

"Ana." E growled, breaking free to rip open her dress, but became aware of the force he was using and went still.

He'd always been a sweet and gentle lover, coveting her body, treating her with the utmost respect. That was so ten years ago. "You better not stop," she ordered, arching her back, letting her lace-clad breasts slip free of the ivory satin of her dress.

Heat flared in his deep-brown eyes and he finished ripping her dress, also borrowed. Kaitlyn had given her a knowing wink and said she didn't expect it back. Cool air drifted over her skin, causing her nipples to pebble further under his sensual inspection. Like a man possessed, he ripped the front of her bra apart and tore her panties, removing the material so she was bare to him.

Reaching for him, he stopped her. "Don't," he choked. "Just let me look. I…This…I never thought I'd see this again. You're so beautiful." He splayed his fingers over her belly, lightly skimming faint stretch marks earned in the last two months of her pregnancy.

Regret crossed his face. "I wish—"

"Don't." This time she needed him to stop. "I know."

Giving a small nod, he kept skimming his fingers further down until he was at her center, parting her folds, using his other hand to spread her legs until she was open before him. Lifting his gaze to meet hers, he waited for her to refuse, and when she didn't, he slid down until his face was settled between her thighs, dipping his tongue into her heat.

A groan escaped her lips and she lifted her hips into him. Using the movement to grab under her legs and pull her close, he licked at her until she was writhing, but keeping her close to the edge, not letting her plummet over.

"E, please." She panted, riding the pleasure, trying to take it all the way. At the sound of his name, he nipped at her bud, shoving her over the precipice she'd been balancing on, screaming her pleasure.

Before she finished the surge of orgasm, he was on his knees, pulling her toward him. He only undid the clasp of his pants, too impatient to remove his clothing. Once he was free, she barely had to time view his thick manhood before he was feeding his length inside of her.

"Ana," he breathed again, falling over her, catching himself with his arms on either side of her head. "You feel amazing, so good."

When she was filled completely, he didn't move, his eyes squeezed shut, body shaking.

"It's okay, E," she urged, realizing she was comfortable with his current identity. He wasn't her husband, he was no longer an Agent, he was just E. "You don't need to be careful with me anymore."

"You're fucking amazing."

With that, he backed out and thrust harder, losing himself in the smooth motion, his thrusts increasing in power and urgency. She held onto his wrists, keeping her knees up and out of the way so he was free to surge back and forth.

Another orgasm built within Ana, his strokes carrying her rapidly to an impending explosion, not stopping even as she rode out another climax, crying her pleasure. He kept his pace, his gaze boring into hers, watching the pleasure build and release, until her voice was hoarse from crying out in ecstasy, until her legs fell limp to each side to use her energy to withstand another earth-shattering wave of bliss.

Sensing she was spent, he arched back, gritting his teeth. "Don't. Want. To. Stop," he bit out, before throwing his head back, roaring her name, and shaking his release within her, where she was still somehow clenched tightly around him. When he collapsed onto her, she let all her inner muscles relax, pried her hands from around his wrists, and lay listless underneath him, enjoying the feeling of his body covering hers.

He abruptly reared up on his elbows. "I didn't hurt you, did I?"

Barely able to keep her eyes open, she murmured, "Absolutely not."

Lightly kissing her eyelids, he slid out from her and curled her into the fortress that was his body. "Get some rest. We're not done yet."

*****

"What the fuck are these?"

Ana drifted awake, partially aware that she was naked and that the furnace she had been snuggled against was no longer there.

"What?" she mumbled, rubbing her eyes.

"These." His fingers traced her backside, and she realized what he might find back there.

"Oh, um." She sat up. They had passed out on top of the still-made bed, leaving her nothing to cover up with. Ana remained bare to him, sitting on the bruises he had been questioning. He had stripped down completely; her eyes widening not at the broad, muscular chest, or the evidence of his arousal, but at the magnitude of marks covering his body. Light beige slashes crossed and puckered his dark body. Scars that had not been there the last time she had seen him naked.

"Ana!" he commanded, lifting her off his magnificent body. "Who hurt you?"

"Well." This wasn't something she wanted to talk about with her husband—oops, mate. But he'd been honest with her. "After you thwarted Griffin's plan to kill our son, he got a little rough with me. The worst was the night before you killed him. I felt almost like he was punishing me for something. He'd never been like that before."

"If I would've known, I would have made him suffer," E seethed.

"I think you did just fine." He clenched his fists, shaking his head like he'd missed his opportunity. Apparently that didn't mollify her mate. "He knew you saved Julio that night. He knew before he died that you were saving both of us. That's revenge enough."

Her words had some impact and he finally softened, appeased. Leaning forward, he firmly cupped both of her breasts in his rough hands. She arched into him, settling her hands over his. It was something she always loved to do: watch his darker skin caress her lighter, caramel-toned body. She'd dated good-looking men, including Griffin. But none of them had shared her heritage like E did. The two of them shared similar upbringings and the deep love of Ana's Nana and E's father. Ana had struggled to remember old recipes and beloved stories of E's mother he had told her to pass down to Julio. Even recalling E's proud, dutiful father enough to pass down a worthy legacy was becoming more of a struggle as each year passed. She feared there'd be nothing left of Julio Senior for young Julio to associate with.

Would E be willing to visit the past, remember what being human was like and the legacy he left behind?

"These are bigger than before." He plumped and weighed her breasts, rolling her nipples between his thumb and forefinger.

"Pregnancy does that to a body." She moaned, the throbbing between her legs increasing in urgency. "How can I feel like this after what we just did?"

Intent on her breasts, he dropped one hand to stroke her center. "Vampires and shifters are horny bastards anyway, but there are many tales in both species of the sexual frenzy after mating."

"And you're a little of both?"

"I'm neither, just finally with the only the woman I've ever wanted to be with."

Melting into him, she shifted and parted her legs, allowing him more room to stroke. "I should be sore. I shouldn't be this turned on," she gasped, between pants.

Drawing her close and raising both of them to their knees on the bed, he continued the circles with his thumb and inserted two fingers into her throbbing channel.

"Ana," he breathed, her heat clamped onto his fingers.

Ana grabbed onto his shoulders to keep from toppling back, not that it would matter, but he was making her feel so exquisite, she didn't want to change anything. Only grab onto his shaft to stroke in a matching rhythm.

A deep rumble emerged from his chest. "So do you like to be spanked?"

"Mmm. What?" Not realizing her eyes had closed as she rode with his movements, they flew open as the question sunk in. "If you try it, you might lose a hand."

E chuckled and hugged her close. "I prefer to grip your sweet ass as I pound into you from behind."

Instantly, he released her, flipped her to her hands and knees, and slammed into her, filling her completely. Her hands grabbed fistfuls of fabric from the bedding to hold onto as he thrust into her. The climb to the pinnacle of euphoria that he had started with his hands was quickly reached as he worked her from behind. Just like before, she reached her peak and toppled over at least two times, her mind too numb to count, before E joined her for the last time, finally emptying himself inside her as her inner muscles milked him completely.

Instead of collapsing on top of her, he climbed off the bed, taking her with him by swinging her up into his arms into the bathroom. He set her down only to turn on the shower.

"I thought we'd get cleaned up. And maybe, if you aren't too sore, our new selves can recreate that night we spent in the hotel after your senior prom."

Her senior prom. God, that felt like it had happened to a different person, in a different lifetime, and in a way, it had. That night, they'd had sex for the first time in the bed, and before she had to be home for curfew, when she was cleaning up in the shower, he'd joined her under the spray and made her an hour late. She'd been grounded for a month by an irate, but resigned Nana.

It had been completely worth it.

"I'm not sore at all."

Chapter Ten

Agent E's defection damaged Madame G's reputation, bruised her pride, and dragged her ego down to the gutter. Dani Santini hadn't been an Agent, but close enough, and she escaped, ruining one of Madame G's greatest accomplishments. Then to have Agent E turn away from Sigma and shed Madame G's taint? That was an event that caught many Agents' notice. A chink in Madame G's armor meant promotion time to some ambitious Agents who sought to take her place and uncloaked a never-before-known retirement option to other withered and worn Agents.

Even recruits, those gossipy bastards, started speculating. Suddenly, they were questioning: did they continue training and being her lackeys if she couldn't even keep her own Agents in line? They had thought that by signing on with the reputed evil master, they'd share in her omnipotence.

Idiots.

Unfortunately, E's escape also put a spotlight on X since, like E, she wasn't recruited but captured and forced into submission. Where before Madame G had little doubt and much use for her two prized steeds, when one broke the fence and bolted, she now had much doubt and limited use for the one left behind.

Now every assignment given to X would be a test. Like sending X to a colony with clans that contained a lot of shifter children. She was under strict orders to capture a few innocent children, albeit temporarily, and encouraged to be brutal enough that the colonies would have to ask for outside help getting their young back in good health. Her actions were meant to draw Guardians away from their headquarters, leaving E and his family vulnerable.

Madame G knew X would balk as she had before when it came to innocents until Madame G had to choose between killing her most prized Agents or finding other uses for them. Her dark mistress suspected X would resist further to aid E's escape and sought to test her allegiance. So X swore to draw the Guardians out from their protective circle. Of course, Madame G sent two sadistic bastards along with to make sure X got the job done.

Now sitting in the car E usually drove, Agent P was at the wheel and Agent A rode in the backseat.

"So Agent X, Agent A and I have a bet," Agent P drawled. He was douche, and she could practically feel his arousal at the prospect of attacking a colony full of young families, anticipating the hunt of terrified females.

"Please tell me PeeWee. I'm dying to hear." X maintained her thousand-yard stare out the window, her mind working on how not to destroy herself during this mission.

Agent P's lip curled at her nickname for him. Score. She always knew what could piss a guy off. "We think that you got your letter name because you cross your feet around E when he's nailing you."

"Or Demetrius," Agent A piped up from the back.

Duuude, never heard that one before, or something along the lines of, "You can't have sex without X." The jokes were only made once. She ensured the same person, and any witnesses, never made them again.

But they were in a moving vehicle, and she'd kill them eventually. "Good one PeeWee, but you got it wrong." She turned to him and in her most seductive purr said, "It's because when I'm done with you, the shape of your dick is an x."

Agent P shifted in his seat, and Agent A cleared his throat. Their tendency for violence against females was legendary. Let them think on that awhile and leave her the fuck alone to figure out the crap stew she found herself in.

She sensed his intention before he made his move, the arousal was almost suffocating in the enclosed space. A hot hand spread across her leg and squeezed down to her inner thigh.

"There's a park up ahead. I think we should stop and you let me and Agent A back there make an x inside of you."

Mental eye roll. Another one she'd never heard before. Pursing her lips as if she was thinking about being the filling in their cream sandwich, X pondered a moment. Agent P just solved one problem for her.

Before he could even move his hand off her leg, she'd drawn her gun from her shoulder holster and fired a shot, point blank, into his head. Agent A yelled and clawed for his own sidearm, but Headshot had been driving and the car was swerving all over the place.

Since they were on a deserted road, X reached over to shove open the driver's door and push the Agent's limp body out. Distant thumps could be heard as the body rolled across the pavement. X calmly crawled into the driver's seat and brought the car to a stop.

"What did you do, you crazy bitch?" Spittle flew out of Agent A's mouth as he clambered for his weapon when he stilled, noticing X still held her gun, and it was pointed at his forehead.

"Respect the X."

Blinking in disbelief, he nodded dumbly, not saying a word. X climbed out, strode toward the prone Agent and hauled him to the trunk of the car. Releasing the latch, it popped open and she dumped the body inside.

Agent A's mouth fell even more agape at her show of force. Stupid Agents. She didn't parade around in her wolf form, rarely changed into it lest Madame G get more ideas for using her, so most Sigma personnel forgot that she was a shifter with shifter strength. P's body was nothing more than nuisance weight.

Silence filled the car as she drove toward the park Agent P had mentioned and parked in the empty lot. Agent A watched from the backseat as X retrieved Agent P's body from the trunk and dumped it in one of the large metal garbage cans at the edge of the parking lot. Agent P was starting to twitch so X made quick work of getting his clothes burning. Then she went back to the car, grabbed her coffee, and as the rest of the perverted Agent's body burned, she held her cup over the flames to get her morning brew nice and hot again.

Overkill?

Perhaps. She sensed Agent A's shock and trepidation at being stuck with her for the next few days. At least she would be able to truthfully report to Madame G that Agent P accosted her, thinking the assignment was permission to use her body at his will, completely disregarding his duties. X could defend herself because she had an important mission to carry out to get E back. Otherwise, her mistress wouldn't care.

Sipping her coffee, she climbed back into the driver's seat and turned back to stare at the pale Agent.

"You gonna ride back there, A-Team, or get in the passenger seat?"

"Wh-where do you want me?" Aww, poor wittle guy. He's never met a female he couldn't throw around before.

She cocked her head and gave him a teasing look. "If you're going to be a good boy and keep your hands to yourself, you can ride up front."

Reluctantly, but rapidly, he got out and slid into the passenger seat.

"There ya go, A-Team. Let's go raise some hell." She flashed him an impish grin, then took another drink of her steaming coffee.

*****

"Come on! It's a game. Who can get to that hill first?" X challenged the two little boys she'd lured away from the small village that was tucked deeply into the wooded hills. "Once you get there, wait for me."

As the brothers ran ahead, competing with each other to see who was the fastest, X treaded steadily behind. They were safe enough, for now.

X and her new partner had arrived late in the afternoon of the previous day after a very peaceful drive. Agent A listened to her plan, and she sensed his excitement as she outlined his duties, which were basically to go in and terrorize the place. He was a fairly new Agent and still brainwashed into thinking shifters were the lesser species after humans. X had to trust the clan leaders could handle the iniquitous Agent before he caused too much damage. And well, if they didn't, tack another load to her already burdened conscience.

Meanwhile, she was to capture children because nothing drew the Guardians faster than threatened young. Protective buggers they were. She had mad skills to keep from being found by the clan members. Because once they were found, she would capture their gaze and turn them right back around, hypnotically convinced they had looked everywhere, the children were lost to them.

She did that all night long as the children slept, turning away five males and one terrified mother. Unfortunately, the terror worked in X's favor and she did nothing to soothe the frantic female, just sent her back to the clan leaders.

Inhaling deeply, X rolled her shoulders and swung her arms before reaching into her pocket and putting some putty in her ears. The male she sensed that was on his way would not be turned away so easily and would relish the fight with her.

"About time you made it, Boo."

Jace Stockwell pulled up short, his pale blue eyes alight with distain, his gleaming ebony gun drawn and trained on her. "Where are they?"

"I'm sorry, who? I'm just out for a walk."

Jace's mouth twitched, animosity pouring off him in waves. While he may have heard she was the aunt of Bennett's mate, and may have suspected she wasn't full-on evil like she wanted everyone to believe, he still held a mighty grudge against her for kidnapping him and his mate, Cassie, then drugging her, and just kinda being a bitch.

"Are they alive?"

X threw him an irritated look. "Ass."

"Tsk, tsk, tsk. Sensitive, Agent X? Tell me where they are."

She shivered against the vibrations from his powerful voice. Shaking her head, she pointed to her ears and spoke loudly and obnoxiously. "Sorry, I can't make out what you're saying."

Before, she'd been mostly reading his lips, his words, muffled. Now, she filled her head with her own static, letting the clay balls do the rest of the work, keeping Jace's resonating voice from influencing her.

Narrowing his eyes, she focused on his nose, or forehead, anywhere but his ice-blue peepers. "You've really grown in power!" She shouted at him, sensing his irritation spike.

"Hand over the kids."

Rolling her eyes skyward, she started singing, her hips shaking. "He-ey Macarena!" Hopefully the little boys didn't hear the ruckus and stayed where she told them to.

Jace practically had to yell over her singing. "Commander Fitzsimmons will finish dealing with the other Agent and be here shortly!"

Relief poured through her and she cut that shit short. Jace didn't need to know she was insanely relieved to hear the clan leaders had captured Agent

A and were holding him until a Guardian could come interrogate and terminate him.

"Let's do this then." Lunging for the massive male, she wasn't worried he'd shoot. He didn't know where the kids were and wouldn't risk a stray bullet. The boys were shifters and would likely heal just fine, but no one wanted to shoot a kid. No one decent, anyway. Despite his sinister looks with his diamond eyes and shaved head, Jace Stockwell was a solid male.

He had barely holstered his gun before bringing up an arm to throw off her kick. With a solid oomph, he staggered back, but recovered quickly, stalking toward her, sliver glinting off the knife he held.

She pulled her own and engaged in a knife fight with the determined male. It could have qualified more as sparring to keep up their skills, than intent to destroy. Apparently he got the memo that no one but Commander Fitzsimmons was to deal with her. The others did only to spare themselves some extra scars, which Jace was doing now.

As she was coming in low for a slash across his side, he managed to surprise her by kicking out and landing a solid blow to her abdomen, flinging her onto her back. A quick back roll and she was up, ready to defend.

But he wasn't advancing and she sensed why. Rhys Fitzsimmons was almost to their location. There they stood, chests heaving, facing each other, waiting. Jace was bleeding from minor cuts on his forearms, and she had a nice gash along her side.

She felt her side to gauge the extent of the cut. Like her, his knife was laced with silver; one more scar to add to her collection. "Huh. I didn't have an autograph from you yet." Digging in her belt, holding her knife ready with her other hand, she tugged out a small bottle and dabbed the wound with saline before the silver toxicity weakened her. Jace's face clouded with consternation, but he followed suit since there was nothing left to do but wait for Rhys.

"Feel better?" she asked sweetly.

He snarled at her before replying. "Yes."

She studied her fingers like she was looking for a broken nail, making sure to only look up to watch his lips move. "It wasn't personal, me kidnapping you and Cassie. And you did save her."

A low growl vibrated off him. "And then she stabbed me in the back thanks to your influence."

X rolled her eyes and huffed. "Ungrateful much? Did it, or did it not, save your ass?"

He flashed some fang at her, too irritated to answer because he knew she was right.

Rhys' masculine scent became much stronger. When he arrived, X and Jace were standing like they were brawling high schoolers waiting for the principle to show up.

"Hey, look who came to the party?" X called to him.

Jace's boss finally came into view. Gawd, he was a stud.

Rhys Fitzsimmons exuded manliness, from his piercing hazel eyes to his strapping stature. If he was a girl, his short, cropped hair would probably be described as deep strawberry-blond, but he was too brawny for that term. His jaw was always tight, the muscle constantly flexing like he was always pissed off—or around her he always was, anyway. His skin took on the reddish-bronze tone gingers often got working in the sun, creating a roughened appearance that was aided by the wide carriage of his shoulders, tapered waist, and heavily-muscled thighs. She was a tall female, six-feet without boots, and he was still half a head taller than her, and she loved it.

She loved the idea of him. The thought that if things were different, she would've had a respectable mate, an honorable male who spent his life defending his species. Then he'd come home and turn that intensity toward her. Those kinds of thoughts could make a red-blooded female go weak in the knees. Too bad Madame G's black blood flowed through her veins.

"Agent X," Rhys replied in his standard clipped tone.

"Two against one, then? Not bad odds." X wiped a trickle of blood from the corner of her lip where Jace's elbow had caught her during their tussle.

"X!" A little voice cut through the trio. "X, did you see it? I won, I won!" One of the boys popped through the trees, skidding to a stop, his eyes going wide at the large males he hadn't known were there.

The second boy appeared, skidding to a halt behind his brother. His eyes went just as wide. "Whoa…Guardians."

Both Guardians looked from the boys to her. She quirked an eyebrow. "This is where I bow out, boys." Granting a stunned Jace a wink, and blowing a somber Rhys a kiss, she trotted away, giving the boys a final wave. "We'll have to hang another time kiddos."

She headed back in the direction of her car, knowing the males wouldn't follow so they could get the boys back. If she torched her wheels and blamed the Guardians, she wouldn't arrive at the compound for at least another day on foot. Another day she wouldn't have to face Madame G's scrutiny. Then she could claim Agent A was too impotent to carry out his duty without getting killed, leaving her to face two armed Guardians alone. After a short battle, she got away, figuring mission completed, and voila, she's an awesome Agent.

Sensing his presence following her, X pulled to a stop. "Can I help you, Rhys?"

"Jace is taking the kids back." He walked until he was about twenty feet away, tree branches shading his features, his expression unreadable. "We dumped your car into a ravine."

Even better. "I could use a long walk. I ate a whole turtle cheesecake last night, and that's like twelve billion extra calories to burn." She wasn't kidding, either. She stopped for some ribeye and somehow the cheesecake ended up in her cart. She was in the middle of slicing herself a piece when she chucked the knife, grabbed a fork, and ate straight from the box. No one said vampire-shifter hybrids couldn't stress eat.

Rhys narrowed his eyes on her, like he knew she wasn't kidding. "E said you might need help feeding."

That was dangerous territory. "Thanks for the offer, but I'd prefer not to get killed smelling like you."

He stalked toward her. "If you didn't overindulge," his eyes flicked down her body and back up to her face, "and spent a day in the woods getting back to the compound, would you still smell too intimately like me? Or just like we'd been fighting."

"You mean like, if a hybrid drinks from a shifter in the middle of the woods, did it really happen?"

He moved closer until he was peering down at her. "What happens in the woods, stays in the woods."

Holy. Shit. "Did you just make a joke? Why, Rhys," she cooed, "I didn't know you had it in you." Her intended tease backfired because her desire was getting uncontrollable around the mouthwatering male. "All jokes aside, I don't know if I can stop drinking from you without stripping you naked and climbing on." His nostrils flared as he inhaled sharply. "And that would be bad for me."

"Would it?" he spoke quietly. "You would have enough time before getting back."

X's brow creased because he didn't understand, and she didn't want to spell it out. But... "I don't want to feel like I'm giving you sex for blood." *I want* us *to be more than a transaction.*

Undaunted, he countered, "I thought there was no us. And we aren't a transaction." *Damn, he heard that?* "You need blood, and I want you only to have mine. If anything else happens, it's you and me and nothing more. I won't mark you until you're ready."

Hell, that'd be a death sentence. It'd be like a bat signal over her head that she belonged to the commander and she'd let him claim her. As for being ready, she refused to entertain the option that she might have a future with this male. It'd cloud what she might need to do to end Madame G.

Holding his wrist up until it caught her attention, like a diamond would for a rich man's trophy wife, he encouraged her. "No sex, but you need to feed. You don't know what you might have to face when you get back."

It was his concern for her well-being that did it. She and E had a close relationship, and they watched out for each other, but Rhys' regard for her well-being was for her alone, not for her endgame.

Licking her lips because she couldn't help herself, she muttered, "Fine." Then she pulled his wrist to her mouth and sunk her fangs in.

The groan Rhys let out couldn't be helped. Full red lips wrapped around his wrist, and he was standing close to his mate. They'd only ever been this close while fighting, never just standing together, soaking in the other's presence.

He was soaking in more than that. Her scent, her voluptuous body that went on for days, and her gentle tugs on his wrist. Rhys was sure his arousal permeated at least a hundred-yard radius through the woods; his shaft was thick and throbbing, damn near making him dizzy. These days he only grew hard after protecting her dreams, surrounding her dream form, and holding her ethereal body close. He'd wake up tenting his bed like he'd done when he was thirteen, and that was a *long* time ago. Then he'd adeptly take care of business in the shower.

How many years had he been doing that? He only remembered his last act of intercourse because of the awful, slimy feeling that had settled deep in his gut because none of the women that night had been *her*. He'd gone on a revenge binge after smelling her intoxicating scent on that arrogant vampire. After that, he couldn't get it up around another female because the interest just wasn't there. Even when he knew X had given her body to another, and it devastated him, he focused on his job and figuring out what his mate was up to.

To be this turned on, in the physical dimension, next to his stunning mate was…exhilarating and erotic and…Another grunt escaped as she tugged on his wrist. Painful. Yep. Exquisite pain thrummed along an invisible cord from where her lips were pressed to where his pulse thrummed in his cock.

The beat crashed through his head; it pounded as his vision clouded. Forcing himself to concentrate, he anchored his other hand behind his back, otherwise, he might start unbuckling her shoulder harness and tactical belt. Hell, just the belt would do, then he could unsnap her leathers and roll them down…

Sweet Mother, that wasn't helping. If he didn't need her to be as strong as possible before returning to Sigma, this would've been a bad idea. Really bad. Instead, he had to think about how he was going to uncross his eyes and not waddle back to the colony sporting a raging hard-on, huffing like a bull in attack mode. He'd wait there after she left and let his body calm down before heading back to meet Jace.

Her strawberry tongue licked over the puncture marks; he almost dropped to his knees with lust. Her tongue had been on him. Her tongue. Licked him. It was better than any shower daydream he'd had, and it fired up all his protective shifter male instincts until they were demanding he take her and mark her and find a way inside her powerful, delectable body.

"Damn," she breathed. "Your blood is amazing. Just…" She drifted off inspecting him. "Rhys, are you all right?"

He nodded, all but busting his teeth clenching his jaw. He finally worked enough words to say, "Go. Before—Go."

Those shocking green eyes of hers narrowed on him, gauging his distress. It almost pushed him over the edge when she chewed her bottom lip with one white fang.

Mercy.

When she started unhooking his pants, he stopped her by putting his hands over hers until she stilled. "Don't. You don't need to. I said I wouldn't." Maybe just touching her warm skin would be enough to see him through the haze of lust.

Tilting her head to consider him, she batted his hands away. "Rhys, how have you lasted this long without going feral?"

Because I found you. Did he say that out loud? He couldn't tell, his mind was clouded in potent desire.

"But we only met in the last decade. You're what? A few hundred years old?"

"Duty," he bit out. "Go."

Her fingers continued to deftly unzip his pants and he lost all breath when her hand wrapped around his length and pulled it out. The cool air shocked his skin, causing his balls to throb.

"I want to do this for you, Rhys. Something I can do for you."

You can survive this crazy plan you have and come home to be with me. She could do that for him.

Sinking to her knees, Rhys looked down, feeling like he had tunnel vision. The beauty down in front of him, with her mouth hovering just inches from his manhood, was all he could see. Sigma could march an army right behind X and he wouldn't notice.

With deliberate slowness, she leaned forward and planted a kiss at the top of his shaft. He hissed like her lips burned him. In all his many, many years, nothing felt as good as that kiss had. Until she slid her lips over him, the heat and moisture of her mouth encompassing his length.

Growling at the magnificent sensation, he forced himself to stay standing while she worked him from tip to hilt, swirling her tongue down and around, up and over. Nearly whimpering as she let him go, his erection bobbed in front of her. She bared her fangs and raked one along a protruding vein. He almost finished right then and there.

Grinning wickedly, she took him back into her mouth and continued her sweet, sensual ministrations. Tunneling his hands through her hair, he moved his hips to the rhythm of her tongue. Rhys loved how the shorn sides of her scalp contrasted with the lush fullness of the top. He stroked her hair, reveling in being able to have his hands on her, treasuring the feel of her instead of pointing a gun at her or slicing her lithe body with a cold blade, but giving her the tenderness and care she deserved.

"Alex, I…I'm going to come." The nickname he'd come to use for her slipped out, and he hoped she didn't mind. It fit her; she was no longer young and sweet Alexandria, and to him she was much more than Agent X.

To prove the moniker pleased her, she hummed over his pulsing shaft, reached into his pants to cup his balls, and he lost it. Going rigid, throwing his head back, he roared into the sky, pumping his load into her over and over and over. He couldn't stop, his voice wore down until he was hoarse, and his strength drained from him after years and years of being a virile male shifter deprived of his mate.

When he was completely spent, she released him from her warm mouth. He sank to his knees, swaying like he was going to collapse.

Surprising him yet again, she tucked him back into his pants and reached up to stroke his cheek. Before he could return the gesture, she was up and gone.

"Boss!" Jace called, running in his direction. "Boss, is everything okay. Whoa!" Jace drew up short, no doubt assailed by the scent of Rhys' climax surrounded by X's aura. "Yeah, so, um…" Jace cleared his throat and turned his back like he was giving the commander a little privacy. "You okay?"

Rhys bobbed his head in a nod, knowing the male wasn't looking, but would sense the movement. Finally, shaking off the mental fog, he heaved to his feet. "Grab the car and meet me down on the highway. I can't have them smelling me and her." And he needed just a few minutes alone, to process what had just happened and with whom.

"Dude, yeah. Okay." Jace started then stopped like he should check on the boss he just caught making what, in his mind, was a massively bad decision. Then he shook his head like he couldn't believe what his senses told him and ran off, following orders.

Good. Jace might not understand yet, but Rhys' mental state was as clear and defined as it could ever be. Any built-up tension from his long bout of abstinence—fuck yeah, gone. Any uncertainties he had—gone. Any concern that X might be lost to him—gone, no matter what she thought. He knew what his duty was now more than ever.

Chapter Eleven

"**Y**ou're doing really well, kiddo," E told Julio, who he was helping scale an embankment.

"Thanks, Dad," Julio said, trying not to show how much the vigorous trek through the thick trees was making him struggle.

E hadn't had much time with the boy since he'd rescued him. The few chances they'd gotten, Julio had seemed shy, but it was better than terrified. Their relationship was new, not exactly traditional, and there was still no guarantee that E, or any of them, would survive. At least Julio knew that he had a father who would go down fighting to the death before he let Sigma have him.

"Is that a wolf?" Julio used the same tone with the overlay of cooool whenever new information was revealed.

"Her name's Irina," Kaitlyn supplied.

She'd been leading the way for them so E could help Ana and Julio make it over the terrain. Once they were clear of the immediate Sigma threat lurking in the woods, she would have to head back to defend the Guardians' quarters. The attacks were becoming more brazen, and despite Dani's upgrades in security, the recruits and Agents were tenacious and would break through the barriers any day now.

E had sensed a female shifter he'd never met was following them, and he wondered how indebted he'd be to the pack when this was all done. "Who's she?"

Kaitlyn fell back so she was closer to E. "Master Bellamy's mate. Irina's a helluva fighter."

"Why didn't she stay back to protect the ones left at the lodge?" Those left behind weren't defenseless by any means, but E hated taking protective resources away from them.

"Well, you trained Dani, and I doubt Dante will let a stranger touch him."

"Whaddya mean?" E asked.

Kaitlyn shrugged, filling him in minimally. "He has some…abilities. If he's not happy, things get wild."

Okaaay. Whatever that means.

"Parrish can fight, he just doesn't have field experience. Kind of the same with Ronnie, but he has a little more training. Doc is there to help. I'm sure he can fight, but I don't know how good he'll be. Cassie took her dad camping out of town to get away until all this is over, and Sarah can shift and fight…and shoot." Kaitlyn laughed to herself like Sarah's shooting was an inside joke. E hadn't seen Bennett's mate shoot, but he witnessed her nearly brain a vampire by swinging her shotgun like a bat.

E's nose tickled and his ears became clogged, like when his mother would shove them full of cotton before he went swimming. Agents never got sick. Was it the mating bond overriding Madame G's bond? He patted his ear with the palm of his hand, needing all of his senses if Sigma turned their pursuit to the woods when they found the Guardians' lodge lacking in what they sought the most.

"How long was it before Dani knew she was clear of Madame G's influence?"

Shaking his head, hoping to bring back the sharpness, he could barely make out Kaitlyn's reply. "It was less than twelve hours. Pretty quickly. Started with a nose bleed." Kaitlyn glanced over at him. "Oh shit."

E swiped under his nose, then stared at his finger in confusion. It was covered in blood and a wet sensation developed above his lip.

"And that's the other reason Irina showed up. In case you become incapacitated, she's going to help keep the other two safe."

A sharp inhale behind them suggested Ana heard their conversation. Did her hearing get more acute with their mating? Was this the beginning of becoming free of Madame G's taint?

Ana's attention had turned toward E and all forward progress had stopped. "What's happening?"

"So there's some good news and some bad news," Kaitlyn started. "The good news is that it looks like the mating ritual is working. Maybe it's overriding Madame G's influence?"

"That's good, really good."

"Yep. Buuut we don't know how bad E'll get."

Ana speculated out loud about the part Kaitlyn hadn't mentioned. "Or if he'll even survive, and what he'll be like if he does?"

Solemnly nodding, Kaitlyn dug out a cloth and tossed it to E, who almost missed it, because his reflexes were sluggish. Aww fuck. It'd better be from shock and not because he was losing his enhancements.

"It's okay," Kaitlyn reassured the group. "We prepared for this. Let's keep moving."

*****

Ana's breath caught as she spied the lush area behind the large outcropping that was to be their home for the night. "It's stunning."

"Mom, can I go swimming?" Julio was nearly undressed before his dad stopped him.

"Let me check it out first."

E moved toward the small pond which was fed by two small waterways creating shallow falls. Ana eyed them covetously. She could really go for a bath, even if it involved rocks for floor mats and leaves for washcloths.

They'd been hiking for three days. E's nosebleed cleared up rather quickly that first day making them question if the mating was a failure in that sense. Kaitlyn had left them after the first day and a half to get back and defend the lodge. According to E, the she-wolf Irina, was still out there, shadowing their movements, searching for signs of Sigma trailing them.

Ana should be exhausted, but she felt amazing, invigorated. In fact, she and E had an unspoken arrangement to proceed at Julio's pace since he was only a kid. Since Ana had become E's mate, her physical skills had improved. Her stamina increased, like she could hike these hills all day for weeks. Her senses were sharper; she knew exactly where singing birds were perched and could even make them out among the throng of leaves. And, um…her libido raged. Following behind E, how his shoulders bunched and tensed when he helped their son over rocky terrain, made her mouth water. Catching his scent the previous night as he moved past her to inspect their shelter, had made her wet like she'd never experienced before. And from the sharp turn of his head and stuttered footstep when he had passed her, he'd noticed. She would've been mortified, if she hadn't been so uncomfortable in her own underwear.

Even the memory threatened to dampen her again, and she couldn't have that; last night was unpleasant enough. *Concentrate, Ana.* Get Julio washed up and settled, then she could clean herself up and maybe feel human again after three days in the woods.

Am I still human? Alarm stopped her in her tracks.

"What's wrong?" E asked sharply, turning away from his inspection of the tiny cave they were to spend the night in, having already cleared the little spring area.

"Nothing," she replied automatically. When he didn't turn back to his inspection, she cursed his perceptiveness. "We can talk about it later." She rolled her eyes toward where Julio finished stripping down to his underwear for a dip.

Mollified slightly, E finished searching the cave. "This doesn't go far into the hillside, but it'll give us adequate shelter. We can bank Julio on each side so he doesn't get too cold sleeping."

Her son hadn't slept well the last two nights of hiking. Their shelters had been little more than giant boulders and one wide ledge. E and Ana had dozed on either side of Julio, but her mate didn't need much sleep and kept watch most of the night.

"I'll get our meal ready while he cleans up."

Yay…Protein bars. They could have no fires, therefore no hunting, since Ana and Julio couldn't eat raw meat. Maybe E could, but Ana didn't ask and didn't really want to know the answer. Sometimes Irina appeared to show them berries and roots that were edible.

Ruefully, Ana shook her head. It wasn't everyday a beautiful, and very naked, female appeared out of nowhere. The first time Ana had screeched. E chuckled because he'd heard the shifter. Bastard. Ana's hearing wasn't acute enough for the female's stealth. Then she'd worried about what her son would see, but quickly dismissed the concern. A bare body was the least disturbing thing he'd witnessed in the last couple of weeks.

After she checked on Julio, she switched with her mate. As they passed, they only gave each other a quick meeting of the eyes, a subtle nod, and changed duties. He watched Julio while she arranged their sleeping situation so they could get themselves fed and settled in for the night.

They hadn't been avoiding each other the entire hike. When the terrain didn't wind him terribly, Julio peppered E with questions, until eventually she spied more and more moments that reminded her of the old Julio Senior. He couldn't refuse to answer Julio's inquiries about his childhood, who his favorite superhero had been, what his grandma and grandpa had been like, and his job as a cop.

Yesterday, there had even been a period where E and Ana were finishing each other's sentences as they were telling the story of how her young husband had tried to fix Nana's lawn mower. It ended when he had disassembled and reassembled the machine, only to have at least two parts and five screws left over.

Their laughter had drifted off, with E peering at her, brow furrowed, like he was afraid of the sweet moments. Afraid Ana would reject him. Ana had just sighed and gazed fondly at little Julio, carrying his sturdy walking stick, trudging through the trees.

That moment, while ending awkwardly, had felt like a gift straight from the heavens. As if her deceased grandmother had said, "Here child. You dreamed, so many nights, of what it would be like to raise your son with his daddy. This one's for you."

Ana threatened to tear up again and instead busied with straightening their sleeping bags. When the guys came back, after Julio dried off and dressed again, they sat and ate their protein bars and drank from a fresh supply of newly-filtered water.

"I think we can camp here until we find signs they're on our trail," E said around a mouthful of granola. "Vampires aren't thrilled about going deep into the woods, they don't like to risk it. I only know of one vampire for sure who can flash this deep into the woods, and I don't think we have to worry about him."

Ana lifted a questioning eyebrow, chewing on her own meager stash of food.

"Demetrius is supposedly Madame G's partner, but I don't think she trusts him." E brought the bar up for another bite and wrapped his arms around his knees. They were sitting on the dirt floor of the compact little cave and Julio was snuggled into his down sleeping bag, snoring softly. "He's actually not a bad guy, just an arrogant prick. I don't know why he's tied up with Sigma, just heard his family is big in the vampire world."

"And you don't think he'll chase us?"

E lifted one broad shoulder in a shrug. "Nah. Others can get here, but they'd have to use a lot of energy to travel this far fast enough to keep out of sunlight. We're small potatoes as far as Sigma goes. Me getting away hurts Madame G's pride, damages her street cred, but we're only important to her and whatever she's planning. The rest of Sigma just wants to control shifters, or wipe them out if they don't succeed." E shook his head and chugged some water. "What Madame G specifically wants, we've never found out."

"Power."

"Most likely." He considered her a moment. "Why do you think that, though?"

"Has she been getting more insane, or has she always been this demented?"

E rolled his head from side to side while Ana admired his chiseled jawline and the flexing cords in his neck. "She's been batshit crazy since I was brought into her world. Stories from other Agents make it sound like she's always been cruel. Modern technology has given her the means to move beyond plain torture to sadistic experimentation.

"Maniacal leaders always want power. Last year, a manager from hell was finally fired. No one had the balls to do it for years, even though every one of us complained. He started doing crazy shit, like taking away our supplies when he'd come in for work before everyone else. Yet, none of upper management batted an eye. Anyway, he was getting violent, and to save their own ass, the bosses started investigating and fired him."

Ana took another bite, giving it a pond water chaser. "So anyway, I felt sorry for him. He never made the jump to the upper echelon and it drove him crazy. Like literally, until he was doing anything and everything that filled his need to feel omnipotent. So maybe Madame G… I mean, she's a female. If she's immortal, or whatever, I can't imagine gender issues are exempt in other species. I mean look at the Guardians, only one female, and I'm sure other packs are like that. How about vampires?"

E's expression was utterly perplexed. "I don't know. I guess she's the only powerful female I've met with fangs. I've been around female vampires," he shivered almost imperceptibly, but Ana caught it, "and they're more powerful than humans. But now that you mention it, when I hear talk of the shifter and vampire leading bodies, they sound mostly male."

Her mind working over the problem, Ana felt like she was in her comfort zone. Her job in research didn't mean she was the grunt who just carried out the testing. Often, the PhDs she worked for bounced theories off the whole office for a wide variety of input. She and E might not be talking about how a drug affects a certain strain of bacteria, but it was still like trying to discover a cause-and-effect relationship. "And if vampires succeed in controlling the shifters, where will that leave Madame G?"

E studied the tips of his boots, deep in thought. "Nowhere different. Still in charge of Freemont's Sigma chapter." He nodded his head slowly. "Unless she orchestrated and controlled the event that took over the shifters. Then she could use them to rule the vampire world. The problem is, we don't know how she's gaining her powers. Shifters all have standard physical abilities over humans, and at least one superior mental ability that varies among them. Vampires are the same physically, and they can flash from one location to another and have some mental powers, especially over humans."

"Because they need to eat." Ana stretched her legs out, trying to ignore how E's dark eyes raked over her limbs. Glancing toward Julio, she found him passed out in his sleeping bag, the last three days of the excursion finally having caught up with him.

"Exactly. They seduce their prey, heal the fang marks, and make them forget. If they're not demented and just kill their meals." E followed Ana's gaze. He never lost the look of awe and pride when he gazed at his son. The fear was still there, too. Fear this would all get taken away from him again. A feeling she shared. "Madame G is different. She can choke someone without laying a finger on them, use spells to bind her blood to another being, and we've even seen her create storms out of a clear sky and direct the lightning."

Ana arched her back and stretched her shoulders, feeling E's heated gaze land on her chest, although her thick long-sleeved shirt and sports bra kept her ladies tucked in nicely. "Like she's stealing power? Can that happen?"

"Dunno." E tore his blazing eyes off her breasts, shifted his position and returned to inspecting his boots. "They say vamps and shifters were created together, and one species chose to follow the light and earthly ways, the other chose to follow a dark-spirited path. Makes sense. Shifters live off the land, calling it Sweet Mother Earth. Vampires have always blended among humans, forced to use them for food. X and I have mulled over if demons really exist. We haven't seen any, but we've seen some pretty sick, twisted stuff. That kind of perversion has to come from somewhere, right?"

Releasing a wry chuckle, Ana threw her hands up. "A couple of weeks ago, I'd probably disagree with you, saying there are good people and bad people. Now that I know humans aren't the lone bipeds on this planet, I'd still disagree with you…to an extent. But after the stories I've heard, and from what I've seen, I'd say that level of evil is getting some help from down below."

"X and I suspect she may have sold her soul," E said softly.

For real? Now they're talking about selling souls? What happened to the days vampires didn't exist and dead husbands didn't come back from the dead? "I guess if we're thinking demons might be real, let's assume selling souls is possible. It would basically be a business transaction. What would a soul get you?"

"If Madame G wanted power, that'd be the price."

"But she's still trying for more power, and although she sounds diabolical, she doesn't sound insane…much. The power she has isn't enough; she's still attempting to get more, more control, more domination. Would she be trying to get another soul to attain the level of power she wants?"

E's brows shot up. "Motherfucker!" he breathed. "She's been trying to tie herself to a shifter baby, implant herself into the baby before it's even born. All of her attempts have been unsuccessful. The only successful insemination was Dani, but her and Mercury's bond pushed Madame G's influence out."

Frowning, Ana pondered the new information. "How can she tie herself to a baby if she has no soul? Didn't the commander say the blood bond ties our souls together?"

"You said to consider it like a business transaction. What if there's some entity that gave her a little extra power up front, and in return, she needed to provide them with…What? She's had plenty of shifter prisoners to trade."

"I'm guessing souls need to be freely given, or in a baby's case, if she tied herself to it, she has the right to give it away."

A thought lightened E's face. "And what if, this evil spirit needs a nice, fresh body? What better way secure her ties to the power source than to be a part of the power?"

"If all those bad sci-fi movies you dragged me to were correct, evil would be free to roam the earth."

E gave a low whistle. "I'm going to find Irina and tell her our theories, let her pass them on to the Guardians." He leaned over and gave her a solid kiss, lingering only for a second, before crawling out of the cave.

Before he disappeared entirely, he turned back. "I always thought your brains were as hot as your body." Then he was gone.

Ana's breath hitched. This was no place to get hot and bothered. Or, it was exactly the place, because she was practically throbbing for him after that searing look he gave her. They'd been tiptoeing around each other while hiking side by side. Neither one had mentioned their mating night when they'd come together so often it put their current relations in a whole separate class from their young, human, naïve sex.

Back then, he'd been so sweet, so romantic, concerned only for her pleasure. He had been her first, and he hadn't had much more experience. They had learned together, laughed at their innocence, and took each other for granted. Maybe that was the biggest difference. After having almost everything ripped away, they both knew what could be lost, and that fueled them ravish each other with abandon. Having increased physical stamina certainly helped—for both of them. Never, never, would he have taken her then like he had on the night they were mated. He wouldn't have lingered between her legs until they were shaking, tears of pleasure streaming down her face. There'd have been no tugging and nibbling on her breasts, and certainly no taking her on her hands and knees with such force that they both slid off the bed. The laughter though—after massively climaxing together on the floor—had been like old times.

Even now, it plucked at her heart. Old times. By far the hardest part of the survival game she found herself in was constantly being reminded of her former married life, when they'd been over the moon happy. Blissfully ignorant of non-human evil in the world, planning her school and their future.

Fondly drawing her hand down her sleeping son's face, she marveled, like eight-thousand times before, at how much her son looked like his father. When her husband had still been thought dead, little Julio's features only prompted memories of his dad's strong jaw, dark eyes that glimmered when upset, and hair that curled tight and thick. But now, she could compare the two side-by-side, and she swore Julio was picking up more and more mannerisms of his father's, even ones that weren't developed ten years ago. Like the tight draw of his shoulders as if he was always expecting an attack, the constant scrutiny of their surroundings, and the lightness in his step that would ready him to spin and attack in less than a heartbeat. He was becoming a Mini Me of E, except for his bright smile, paired with a dimple that Ana could claim came from her.

She was bombarded with her son and his father being reunited. But E was not her late husband, yet he was. And she wasn't the Ana of ten years ago, either. And they were mated now, not married. Technically, if he didn't die then the death certificate was null and void. Right? Or does more than ten years give it a level of permanence? Ana gave her head a shake. It was mind-boggling, and she'd had enough unbelievable moments lately.

A dip in the little wannabe lake would be nice, and maybe she could pretend it wasn't frigid and muddy.

Ana made her way to the waterside. Shucking her boots off when the ground became squishy, she stripped off all her clothing, but took her knife and only one gun with her as she headed to the water. Who knew she'd be comfortable as a walking arsenal? Could she even go back to the real world? Measure out drugs and chemicals for testing, gossip in the break room, and not think about her son getting attacked while she was at work, not feel the solid weight of the side arms strapped to her hip, and the blades harnessed around her legs?

Wading into the water, she paused long enough to let her ankles get used to the chilly water swirling over her feet. Not as icy as she feared, but cold enough deep in the woods, in early fall, to make a person pause. It would be the cold shower she needed after witnessing E's strong, capable body maneuver the terrain, safeguard their son, and rest only a foot away. Not to mention his unique male scent wrapping her in comfort until daybreak as they both lent their warmth to Julio during the brisk nights.

She waded in further, steeling herself until she could sink down into a crouch with her shoulders in the water. Okay, there would be no lingering, it was too chilly. Quickly scrubbing sweat and dirt off her face and out of her scalp, she decided against a full wet head until the sun was out. If they were going to hide out here a while, then a wet head at high noon would be more comfortable and dry faster.

She rose, grabbed her weapons off the large rock she found to use for a shelf, and moved nimbly over little sharp rocks, on her way to the shore. Scurrying to her pile of clothes, she put her knife and gun back into their holsters, noticing too late, the dark figure waiting thirty feet away in the trees.

"I thought you'd be gone for a bit," she said nervously, straightening and resisting the urge to cover herself.

His stance portrayed nonchalance leaning against a tree trunk, but his gaze burned as they trailed the water droplets over her chest, between her breasts, and down her belly, to run between her legs and drip to the ground. "I *was* gone for a bit."

Ana made no move forward. "What'd Irina say?" Like talking business was going to dampen the desire between them.

Intensity flared from him as he eyed her taut nipples, jutting out from the chill at first, but now it was like they were straining to get to the intent male. They weren't the only ones. It was all Ana could do to stay in place, and she had yet to come up with a valid reason why they shouldn't indulge in each other's bodies.

Julio was with them. But he was in a deep sleep.

They were on the run for their lives, but there were possibly days of reprieve where they could rest and wait.

She didn't want to get close to the Agent only to lose him. *Screw it, take him while you can, as often as you can.*

Irina was still out there, and it'd be embarrassing if she heard them. Yeah, that was good enough.

"She said they had come to some of the same conclusions, but hearing similar theories from us, filled in with the information I gave them, made their assumptions more valid. Maybe they can start to plan an offense instead of always being on the defense." Daylight was gone, but she could sense blistering emotion rolling off the male she was facing nude. "Come here."

"We shouldn't."

"Why not?"

Because…why? Oh yes, the female shifter. "Irina's out there."

The corner of E's mouth quirked up. "She headed back to get more supplies for us. Kaitlyn's going to meet her halfway. We thought it was safe for her to be gone a day."

Ana blew out a breath. There goes her defense. "Come here."

Uncertainty welled up, with a dash of shyness. This wasn't survival, they had already mated. This would be for pleasure only. "I don't know…"

His eyes narrowed on her, and she felt like she was timid prey that had a spotlight illuminating her. "You are mine, Ana."

"For how long?" Anguish coated her words. Didn't he see? Losing him again would rip her apart.

He started forward, and she commiserated with the bunnies that would go after Nana's sugar snap peas. She now knew exactly why they froze in plain sight as soon they heard someone walk out onto the tiny porch facing Nana's treasured garden. For a few seconds, they could pretend they weren't seen by a passing predator, fooling themselves that their brown fuzziness wouldn't be obvious against the green grass. Standing nude, the cool night air evaporating droplets off her skin, making it pebble from the chill, she was frozen, irrationally hoping E would pass her by. Because if he didn't, and he swept her up in another maelstrom of passion, she'd be that much more devastated if she lost him.

Every time he talked, it suggested he was tangible, that her mind didn't create this wild fantasy from deep-seated longing. Each time he interacted with their son, he was the father she'd wished for Julio his entire life. Every touch, every kiss, every conversation, made him a man again. Not enhanced, not an Agent, not a rugged male who used to be her husband, but a man. A man she could easily fall in love in with…again.

"You're mine as long as I can keep you. I'm not wasting any time we have together." He stood over her now. The heat radiated off his body, warming her chilled skin.

Looking up at him, she wanted nothing more than to lose herself in his embrace. "I don't want to lose you again. I've dealt with losing my husband, and it almost destroyed me. Now I'm falling for you, and our chances at a happy ending are small."

How could this end well? A psycho with a load of resources was chasing them because her prime male specimen ran off and now she wanted all three of them.

She'd gotten used to E showing little emotion, unlike his former self who displayed his love and dedication regularly.

His face fell. "Ana, I can't claim to know what you went through. I wish I could take it all away, go back to being an ignorant fuck chasing junkies and pulling over speeders. What I did learn is to cherish any moment of pleasure. Which for me, was joking around with my partner, watching you live your completely normal life every day, and raising our son into a young man any father would be proud of."

Ana blinked rapidly at the tears his words wrung out. Before she could respond, he continued. "Your normal life was taken away, and it was replaced by me and danger. But I've gotta tell you, Ana, each day since I've gotten you back, I've experienced more moments to treasure than my entire time without you. Yes, you might lose me again. I might lose you, too, and I can't even think about living without that sleeping boy in the cave. So I will take any moment, any scrap of attention you want to give me, because that's what's worth living for."

Cupping his face, she no longer felt cold; his words warmed her completely. Her Julio, Julio Senior, would have never made himself so vulnerable to her. This man, the damaged warrior standing in front of her, existed only because of her. Even before he found out he had a child to protect, he had committed to living a nightmare for her. How could she not let herself be with a man like this for as long as she was given?

Tracing his lips with her thumbs, she brought his head down toward hers. "Oh my darling Agent E, you are right. Let's not waste another second together."

He held back, reserved, kissing her tenderly, until she pressed into him. "You're cold," he growled, wrapping her tightly in his arms.

"Not anymore," she muttered against his mouth.

He grunted an indistinguishable word and released her so he could shrug his shirt off and drape it over her shoulders. Enveloped in his heat and scent, presented with his bare chest, she trailed kisses over his pecs and down his belly, while working his pants free and down his hips. Before she could do anything with the steel package jutting from above his waistband, he lifted her up into his arms.

"I can't wait," he rasped, lifting her legs around his waist. "It's been three days, *three days*, of watching that ass sway in front of me, not being able to touch you."

"*My* ass?" Ana gasped as he settled her onto his length and she slid down. "Have you seen how tight yours looks in those pants?"

When she was deliciously filled with her mate, she enjoyed it for a moment before rising up and sliding back down. E moaned and dropped his head back, gripping her butt harder, urging her to ride him.

Her hands were clenched around his upper arms, hanging on as he took over. His biceps flexed as he was pumping her up and down. She loved their strength, the way his umber skin defined each striation. Running her hands over them to his chest, up to his brawny shoulders, she hugged firmly into him, her impending release racing to fruition.

He worked her faster, pumping harder. It wouldn't take long to reach a crescendo that would have her wailing her ecstasy into the night. Instead, she bit her lip, tasting the metallic blood, knowing it wouldn't be enough. Since she couldn't yell out into the night and wake her son, and alert every other creature in the night to their location, she dropped her head into the crook of his thick neck. When her orgasm hit, it hit hard. Biting down, she screamed into his shoulder, muffling the sound until she was spent.

E was still thrusting into her slick heat, grunting with the strain of keeping his climax at bay until she had finished hers. Releasing the hold her mouth had on him, she instinctively let her head loll to the side. Following her lead, he buried his face into her neck and held her close, the sting of teeth punctured her skin before another wave of pleasure rolled through her. E's body jacked tight, lunging into her in two long, drawn out thrusts, his grip jerking as he spent himself within her.

"Oh damn," he said, pulling away from her neck. "Did I hurt you?"

While not the most romantic postcoital words, his concern was endearing. "What I was feeling wasn't pain."

"I think I drew blood." Leaning back down, she felt him sensually lick along her collar line. "Mmm, most definitely." He gave her a few more licks, hardening within her again. "Maybe I'm more vampire than I thought. I could drink you dry."

God, his tongue plus teeth at her throat equaled hot. "I might be vampire, too. I think I bit into you pretty hard."

"Good." Abruptly, he withdrew from her and still holding her, gently kneeled down, positioning her on her hands and knees in front of him. "I know you need to get some rest. Just give me one more time." Pushing into her, she closed her eyes and leaned back into him.

"All right. Only once or twice more."

His deep chuckle was all she heard before getting lost in pleasure under the canopy of leaves.

Chapter Twelve

Languidly stretching, E realized it had to be nearly sunset. Shit! He popped up, but remembered to stoop before knocking himself out on the roof of the cave. A dart of fear hit him in the chest as he realized he left his family alone and undefended.

Blinking in the fading daylight, he didn't relax until he saw Ana and Julio sitting at the base of a large tree, playing tic-tac-toe in the dirt. Or it looked like maybe it started that way, but now his boy was drawing a crude outline of a castle, spewing theories of what the best defenses would be, and how an army of trolls could still breach said defenses.

Ana's eyes twinkled with amusement when she glanced up, and her face broke out in a knowing smile. What they'd done before he let her get some rest had been explosive, spectacular. It was even better than their mating frenzy, because the need was all for her and not a way to cement their bond. Likewise in the way she responded to him. She'd been wet and ready for his entrance with no preparation, her explosions had been nearly instantaneous. It made a man feel powerful.

Since she had spent herself completely, he had stayed awake for when Julio woke up in the morning and just hung out, chatting with the boy until Ana had risen. Then it was E's turn for a short rest. Today would mark the best day of his life.

Julio glanced up. "Oh, hey Dad." He went back to his diagram. "See Mom, if they're not giant trolls, then a moat would work and maybe it could be stocked with, like, piranhas, or...or acid."

E marveled over his son's imagination. When he was a kid himself, he was into jumping ramps with his bike, playing soccer, or maybe a game of marbles once in a while. Ana had been all toy microscopes and threading bead bracelets. But this kid was something else, collecting cards and fantasy worlds. Was *Star Trek* still playing? Because Julio was a prime demographic to Trekkie the hell out. For a brief moment, E mused at how it might have been different had he been around, if the outcome would have been better or worse. Or just different. No matter what, his kid was fucking fantastic. Maybe there was still time to get him interested in soccer.

Three short yowls, followed by a long howl broke out off in the distance. E stilled, a pit forming in his stomach.

Ana's demeanor instantly became cautious, rising to a stand, bringing Julio with her.

"That was Irina." E scanned their campsite, looking for anything needing to be packed before they took off.

"She must've been on her way back and sensed Agents. How did they find us so fast?" His mate's voice was strong and steady. She was a hell of a woman.

Cursing that his enhanced abilities didn't include telepathy, he could only conclude that Irina was following their previously arranged warning system: three barks for three Agents, and from the yowl, they were vampires. Madame G knew they were on the run and sent two vampires to take care of him, and an extra to finish the job and deal with his wife and son.

"The mating must not have worked. Madame G can still sense me, and she sent vampires willing to risk the distance. Get in the cave, push Julio to the back, and arm yourself."

Ana and Julio were scrambling past him when his son pulled up short, squinting through the shadows. "Your nose. It's bleeding."

"Again?" It hadn't bled more than the tiny trickle the day after they had mated. Bringing his finger up, yep, the kid was right. Fuck! It would be like spraying *eau de parfum* all over their campsite. He might as well hang chemlites all over to light it up, too. Hell, why not start a fire and roast marshmallows? The fangers already had an approximate location to start hunting, now they could pinpoint him and be there within minutes.

Any daylight left peeking over the horizon was rapidly fading, hindered even more by the thick trees, hence the reason why the vampires could get an early start hunting. Flashing through the trees would limit their exposure to the sun's rays. But as daylight was becoming a memory, the vamps would be able to utilize their speed and reach their location easily.

After urging Julio into the cave, Ana turned back. Her eyesight having sharpened since mating him, she said, "E, your eyes look bloodshot. Are they *bleeding*?"

What the hell? Touching a fingertip to the corner of his eye then rubbing his thumb over the pad, foreboding filled him.

"Why now?" he muttered.

"Was it something we did last night? I mean," she lowered her voice so Julio wouldn't hear, "we both bit each other."

"And drew blood. Son of a bitch! We had a mating ceremony and mated like shifters, then last night we mated like vampires."

"What's going to happen?" She sounded terrified, like she had complete faith in E, but if he became incapacitated, all would be lost. And it would be. She wasn't a wimp, but would be no match against vampires.

"We follow our plan. Make sure Julio has sharpened sticks to use for stakes and his knife. You defend the cave, I'll defend you."

He gave her his back to gauge their surroundings. That was when his ears tickled. Oh hell, was he leaking from every orifice? Deftly touching the inside of one ear answered his question. He paced, tearing a portion of his shirt to use as a rag so he would limit the blood spread. What bad fucking timing. One more day was all they needed. He could've bled his little heart out, and hopefully survived and recovered. Then they could've made their way to another site to camp, and Madame G wouldn't have been able to hone in on their position. They could've just waited. Waited until she lost interest, gave up, or even better, got killed by X and the Guardians.

The Agents were close. His belly tightened, and maybe it was nerves from anticipating the fight.

Nope. Cramps were building in pressure until waves of nausea rolled through his gut. Perfect.

"Get ready," he snarled, sensing the impending arrival. Ana drew her gun in her right hand and pull a knife into her left. If his ears weren't ringing, he could probably even hear the hammer of her heartbeat.

"Agent E!" boasted one of the Agents who was first to arrive. "I must say, you smell delicious."

What was his letter? Z? No, R. Z was further back in the trees, staying out of sight with the third, a female. O was her designation and she was a flat-out bitch.

"I'm going to look forward to this," she taunted from her hiding spot.

"Come get some, bitch," he shot back.

"Oooh look," Agent R said, crouching to spring on him, "he's already marinating for us."

Sadly, the Agent was right. E was now bleeding profusely from his nose, and the cramps were increasing in pain and power until he wanted to crash to his knees and curl up in a ball to ride out the excruciating twisting in his gut.

Oh hey, that's pretty much what he did. Doubling over, he heaved with enough force that he expected to see his liver sitting on a crusty pile of leaves on the ground. Heaving again, he spit out mouthfuls of thick, red mucus. Dropping to the ground, he gave himself over to the retching.

Agent R was taken off guard by the turn of events and Ana took advantage of the lull.

A shot rang out and rage crossed the vampire's face as red bloomed across his chest. He bared his fangs, hissing toward where Ana was hidden. "You'll regret that, little human."

The vampire used his unnatural speed to get around E, who, heaving, tried to reach out and trip up the Agent before he reached Ana. His reflexes were too slow and sluggish, he missed, but a light-colored blur sped by him and tackled the Agent. Growling and scuffling, Irina and the Agent rolled and ripped at each other with their fangs.

Nut up. E heaved himself to his knees. *Let the blood flow*. Blinking his vision somewhat clear of the bloody haze, he yanked a gun out with each hand. His eyesight was shit, his hearing dulled, his nose was worse than a leaky faucet, and the cramps threatened to make him face-plant again, but he'd take down as many of these bastards as he could so Ana and Julio could get away.

Through the curtain of red, he saw a lithe form appear on his right. Agent O stalked him, taunting him. "You're not doing too well, Agent E. You should rest. Let me help you out."

Raising his arm to fire at her, a sudden sharp prick stung in his side.

Tranqed. He was an easy target in his condition, but if they tranqed Irina, then Ana and Julio would be in trouble.

A sudden gasp from Ana, followed by the thud of her gun, made E even sicker to his stomach. The Agents' aim with their tranq guns rang true. He swooned on his knees, straining to focus through the trees and take out more Agents before they got to his boy.

"Mom!" Julio's terrified voice rang out. "Mom!"

"Stay down son," E said, or at least tried to, his words coming out in a slur. What came out was some blood-tinged spittle and guttural noises.

Struggling to stand, E squinted through a red haze to make out his son draped over a sleeping Ana. His eyes darted around to find Irina, only to see the shifter fall away from the Agent she was battling, a red dart in her flank.

With one final heave, E almost cleared the ground, but he was no match in his condition against the powerful drugs. His body seized and he fell forward, the red haze turning to blackness.

*****

"Stand down, Dane." Commander Fitzsimmons crossed his arms over his broad chest and stared down the frantic male.

"Easy for you to say, Rhys." Dane Bellamy ripped his stare away, ran his hands through his salt and pepper hair, and stalked back and forth in front of the lodge. "It's not your mate they captured." Back and forth. "It's not your mate they'll torture and humiliate."

The commander kept his arms crossed, saying nothing, waiting for Dane's own words to sink into the male's thick skull.

Dane stopped, blowing out a gusty breath. "Fuck, Rhys. I'm sorry."

It wasn't exactly a well-kept secret within his pack that Agent X should've been his mate. His fellow Guardians had mostly figured it out, seeing evidence of how territorial he'd become in his dealings with the infuriating female, and his declining-to-nonexistent visits to the club most shifters went to deal with their pent up sexual aggression.

Dani had discovered the picture of X, and that's when the reality of who she was, what she'd been put through, and how much they both had to lose in the battle with Madame G had sunk in. If they could

~159~

get through all that, and Rhys could somehow free X and mate with her—a near impossibility by itself—they would have an even bigger problem to face.

She was a hybrid. A hybrid who would have to orchestrate the power struggle between vampire leadership and his Lycan Council. A female who would refuse to be ruled by either governing body, not after her years with Sigma, and would die to keep her family free of domination, or worse, eradication, by either governing body.

"The twins are on their way," Rhys assured his longtime friend. "The dawn after they arrive, we attack."

"When the vampires are at their weakest?"

Rhys nodded grimly. They needed the numbers, so he called the twin Guardians back from their unofficial investigation into the leading body of the shifter species.

Boss, Dani says we have a visitor asking permission to enter. Mercury's voice floated through his mind. *Says the name's Demetrius.*

"What the fuck?" Rhys blurted out, before his mind warned him he was saying it out loud. Dane raised his eyebrows, but remained silent.

Tell her no and give me his location. I'll go meet him.

This Demetrius claims to have Irina. Once he's done meeting with you, he'll give you her location. Think it's a trap?

Doubt it. He and Demetrius had a history, sort of. The other shifters weren't as familiar with the vampire who was supposedly Madame G's partner. The vampire leaders had sent him to Freemont to keep tabs on the dark mistress, but all he did was party and chase tail.

Rhys met him one night when he'd been pursuing a suspected Agent in a local club. He had stopped short, Agent forgotten, when he ran across the vampire because that fucking male had carried *her* scent, which meant one thing—sex. He almost went into a rage, intending to kill the vampire. But the Agent he'd been chasing, nailed him in the shoulder with a bullet, slowing him enough that the laughing Demetrius flashed away.

That wasn't the only time he'd smelled his mate on the vampire, and then the bastard had to go and hint as to the reason behind his relationship with X, a claim recently supported by Agent E.

Rhys hated Demetrius. But he didn't. In a way, the party-boy vampire helped his should-be mate. Unfortunately, he did it with his body and that made Rhys' fangs throb. He wanted to rip out the arrogant vampire's throat, tie the trachea around Demetrius' dick, and tighten it until the vile thing fell off.

Alas, he had to act professional, calm Dane, and save Irina. Time to go see what the fang-burdened a-hole wanted.

Chapter Thirteen

His head pounded, his muscles felt like lead weights, and his eyes were crusted shut. Groaning, E tried rolling onto his side, deciding a fetal position might not be a bad thing, but found himself shackled at each limb to a gurney.

He searched for his last memory, trying to defog his mind. There were problems at Sigma, his wife—

Ana! Julio!

E pried his eyes open and waited for the room to quit spinning. Oh wait, the room was holding still, his mind was taking a ride on the tilt-a-whirl. Blinking rapidly, E cleared his vision and looked around.

He wasn't in his own room, no big surprise. He felt…good…excellent. A little weak from blood loss, but he was rapidly recovering. No sickness welling up from his gut, no more blood leaking from orifices. Bonus. Covered in dirt and grime, it looked like he was just thrown into the cell and left alone.

Madame G would know he was no longer tied to her, he'd bled out her essence. So why wasn't he going through round two of what she did to him ten years ago? Most likely she wanted him to witness, and suffer through, what she planned for his wife and son.

His mind ran through scenarios of what she had planned for his family, none of it palatable. E scanned the room for something he could use to test his strength. The doc at the lodge thought he'd retain his enhancements for the most part. He'd need them to save Ana and Julio. *If* he could save them.

Metal clunked and E stilled. Malevolent foreboding preceded the entrance of the dark lady who had ruled his life.

The tall Asian beauty floated in, her floor-length kimono making it appear as if she didn't move a muscle, just levitated a few inches off the floor. Her ebony eyes assessed his demeanor. She didn't need guards or weapons and wasn't concerned about an impending attack. She could stop him in his tracks, cut off his air supply at whim, squash him like a bug.

Her powers seemed all encompassing, and from what well she drew them from, he and X hadn't yet figured out. It was the reason they hadn't—couldn't—make a move to annihilate her. Her mental powers were staggering and unheard of.

"Agent E," her smooth voice intoned, "I'm so disappointed in you."

He remained silent, waiting for her to continue, maybe reveal her intentions.

Instead, she cocked her head to the side, regarding him quietly for a long moment. "You were one of my best Agents. I gave you freedom, and you betrayed me."

Freedom? He wanted to say so much to her, tell her he never betrayed her—he was never on her side to begin with. But anything he said would get taken out on his family. "You didn't leave them alone. That was part of our deal. All you had to do was leave them alone."

The madam's almond-shaped eyes lifted in surprise. Busted. She got greedy and she knew it. "I assumed your boy would have as much potential as you, but Agent G wanted him out of the way before he married your wife." She shrugged one delicate shoulder. "No matter. Your son will be your replacement, and you'll be my guest here." her voice dropped low, menacing. "You can watch all the uses I have for your wife. Unless…you agree to work for me again. Then I'll take pity on poor Ana."

E forced his rage down, debating whether he should beg, bargain, or play dumb until he came up with an escape plan. He didn't get a chance to do any of those things. Madame G gave him one more embittered look and swept out.

*****

The click of the lock alerted E to another visitor. To whom did he owe the pleasure to today?

After a subtle inhale to absorb the scent, he wasn't surprised to see their new doctor and researcher. After Dani's mate Mercury was held captive, and subsequently killed their last mad doctor, E's wicked mistress readily found another replacement. This one was a young female who relished the chance to have free rein studying other species. Where she might have balked at performing her insane experiments on humans, she seemed to revel in the torture of the non-human types, personally carrying out her sampling and testing with certain zeal. Once she saw the results, well…bring on the humans.

Flicking his eyes open to watch Dr. Hansel approach, he steadied his surprise at the activity behind the young doctor. He watched the petite doctor, allowing nothing to change on his face, while letting his peripheral vision take in the slender fingers that wrapped around the edge of the door, holding it open before it shut. The tall figure with the faux hawk soundlessly slid inside before letting the door close behind her.

What the fuck was his partner thinking? All these years and she was putting their hard wrought plan in jeopardy.

"What's the word, Doc?" He had to keep the woman's attention toward him and not behind her. The doctor's human ears might not pick up on the presence of his partner immediately, but the room was small. It would only be a short minute before X was discovered.

"Dr. Hansel," the young physician corrected him in her professional, clipped tone. "You're an interesting case, Agent E. I've been studying your samples, comparing your current blood work to your pre-mated results, and also to other Agents still under Madame G's influence. The results are very interesting indeed." She tapped a pen to her chin, looking over the data on the clipboard she carried.

With the doctor's attention off him, he lifted a brow at X. She jutted her chin, then shimmied her shoulders, like she did when she sang the song she got his nickname Biggie from. His partner could be a real ass sometimes.

Guess they were playing the get-as-much-information-as-you-can-before-killing-the-bad-guy game. "How interesting am I, Doc?"

"Dr. Hansel," she repeated, slightly more irritated. Then she sighed, like why bother explaining anything to him when it'd be like describing rocket science to a housecat. Countdown to giving in to the ego in three, two, one… "Agent E, your DNA profile closely matches your initial profile—the sample they took when they apprehended you." What a bitch. Like the public had been saved getting him off the streets. "However, now you're missing the bands we assume tie all the Agents Madame G has created together."

Paging through the papers clipped to her board, her brow furrowed and she shook her head. "You still have the bands representing the extra genetic material that your body incorporated into its own to enhance your humanness. Now I can start determining which genes get integrated and what abilities they code for."

"How would you do that?" Experimentation, torture, more kidnappings to provide her test subjects.

Dr. Hansel blinked her owlish gray eyes, excitement growing. "Using the subjects I already have, I can isolate the individual genes and inoculate a fresh subject. From there, we'd just wait and see." Setting down her clipboard and pen on the medical-grade tool box next to him, she opened a drawer to don a pair of gloves, then began taking out various tubes and syringes. "If they survive, it'd be as simple as monitoring what ability goes with which gene."

If they survived. The doctor had no qualms using "fresh" subjects, which meant human women, children, and average Joes who had the misfortune of being in the wrong place at the wrong time. Not to mention she'd euthanize each subject after their useful life was over.

X floated across the room and grabbed the mad doctor around the neck, her hand over Dr. Hansel's mouth. There was a flash of surprise in those studious gray orbs, followed by intense pain as X slid a knife through her ribs into the doctor's heart, effectively stopping its beat. When the young woman went limp, X carefully lowered her to the floor and cleaned her blade on the lab coat.

"Do I even need to mention how epically stupid you're being?" E patiently waited for X to undo his shackles, torn between slapping some sense into her and hugging her, thankful for the chance to rescue Ana and Julio.

"I love hearing how epic I am." When E sat up, rubbing his wrists, she hung back, hands on her hips. "I ignored a lot of my better judgment to stick to our goals of ending Madame G. I have enough innocent blood I didn't spill on my conscience. I'm not standing by while she destroys your wife and mutates your kid. And hey, good call on hiding with the Guardians. I bet it took a massive set of brass balls to march up to their door and ask for help."

E lifted his shoulders in a stiff shrug, looking over his clothing still dusted with dried blood. "Needed to be done. Do you know how Madame G found out so fast?"

"Same mysterious way she always finds out shit. I don't think anyone would've thought you'd go there. Or that they'd take you in."

True that. "You gonna run with us?" He knew the answer but asked anyway.

X grimly shook her head. "Nah. She'll beat the crap outta me, but I'll stay. She has to expect my disobedience when it comes to you, and especially Ana and Julio. But she won't kill me."

"She might very well kill you for this."

"Doubt it. She needs to terrorize me to make herself feel better, needs me to show everyone that she still controls me even she if lost you. If I run, I lose the chance to get in close."

Holding out his hand, he turned up his wrist. "You need to feed before she gets hold of you."

X's faced paled and she looked like she was going to puke. "Yeah, you're right." But when she only stood dubiously eying his offered vein, he dropped his hand.

"What's wrong? Are you sick or something?" Then his eyes widened. "Is it my mating? Does that ruin the appetite?"

X shook her head, attempting to brush it off. "Yeah, you're too sweet now. Back off of the donuts."

"Bullshit. What is it?"

X eyed his wrist one more time, then crinkled her nose. "I'm guessing my other side has reared its ugly head. I drank from…" She couldn't finish, anxious about saying any of it out loud. "Whatever. You're still a little low on the hemoglobin levels, anyway."

Other side?

Vampire.

Drank from who?

Ah. Her true mate. He was too impressed that the brooding Guardian got X to tap his vein to be shocked. Full-blooded vampires couldn't be with anyone else physically once they encountered their true mates, unlike shifters. They could drink from others, but it often made them sick. X was only a half-blooded vampire and the no sex rule hadn't pertained to her, but maybe blood was different. There wasn't enough known about hybrids.

Standing, E worked the kinks out of his neck and back from being prone so long. "Now it's even more dangerous for you to stay."

"Yep." Otherwise ignoring him, she continued. "They've got Ana in the fangbanger rooms. They're enhancing her so she'll survive being used as recreation." Rage pounded at E to get to his mate as soon as possible, but he forced himself to hear X out. "Julio is across the compound. They plan to convert him and study how he grows into his powers. You go get Ana. I'm sure they've pumped her full of sex drugs, so it won't be as awkward if she jumps your bones. I'll get Julio out."

"Us against the world?" How in the hell were he and X going to get Ana and Julio out of their holdings, out of the compound, and then get them to safety? Maybe if they got to freedom, *if*, they'd have a chance this time since he was no longer cosmically tied to the madam.

X's mouth curved into a ghost of a smile. "Rumor has it the compound is going to be under attack any moment." She shot him a grin with a rare flash of fang. "Ready to party?"

"The Guardians are coming for us?"

"You must've made quite an impression."

E grunted. "They fucking love me. Did your information leak happen to say when exactly?" E needed to get to Ana before another male did.

Then he heard it. A muffled boom followed by the walls rattling.

"That's our signal." X lifted the doctor's cooling hand, while E found a scalpel to secure one of her fingers. They'd need her digit to open the door so it'd look like only the doctor entered and left his room. Hopefully, whoever was watching the cameras were intent on the shifters' attack.

Tucking the severed finger into his pocket, knowing his prints would access a whole lot of nothing after his defection, he and X parted ways at the end of the corridor. Blasts to the exterior walls shook through the buildings. Thanks to the attack, there were no Agents in the lower levels, and hopefully none servicing his mate.

His jaw ached from grinding his teeth, and he forced himself from an all-out sprint. He needed to get to Ana without incident before he could save her. Swiftly maneuvering through the corridors, he made it to her room and heard a commotion inside.

"Leave me alone!" his mate raged.

Sidling up to the long rectangular window in the door, he peeked inside. A nearly naked male circled Ana, who was nude, flushed, and swinging a metal leg she'd ripped off a rolling nightstand. Guess her strength had increased.

The male's back was to the door. His shirt was off, his pants undone, and Ana was backed into a corner. Blood splattered the walls and floor, but little was on Ana. She must've gotten in some serious hits, catching the male by surprise before he opted to keep his distance.

In awe, E watched as the male lunged for his terrified, but extremely pissed off mate. She flew under his reach, catching the male with a solid strike to the torso and backed into another corner to defend herself before he could disarm her. Looked like her speed was coming along quite well, too.

E remembered the day he woke up after his capture. He'd been under for weeks, adapting to the chemicals and blood concoctions that had been administered, and recovering from the injuries he had obtained while getting abducted. When he finally came to, he had no sense of who he was and was helpless against his driving needs.

Ana had been taken three days ago. Had she just woken up? The conversion process didn't act that rapidly. Only three days? Watching Ana fend for herself with amazing speed and reflexes, he wondered if their mating had made the conversion go more smoothly. Before capture, her natural senses were increasing in acuity, like human mates of shifters.

E waited for the male to make another move for Ana before he used Dr. Hansel's finger to open the door. He stalked inside as Ana's batting hand was yanked by the male, and she was dragged closer.

Gliding up behind him, E grabbed the male, a recruit from the smell of him, around the throat, and pulled and twisted until he heard the signature snapping that accompanied a broken neck.

Ana gasped and as soon as the male's hand slid limply from her arm, she raised her weapon to brain E.

"Ana!" E raised his forearm to protect his head from her beating. It wouldn't kill him, but it certainly would incapacitate him.

"E!" Dropping the mangled metal, she jumped into his arms, smashing her mouth into his.

At her unexpected reaction, he stumbled back, recovering to her lifting his shirt, trying to get his clothes off. Fucking libido drugs.

"Ana." Setting her down, he tried to keep her from undoing his pants, and as appealing as a certain appendage of his found her actions, he wouldn't let it go that far. "Ana, stop!"

She stalled and blinked up at him. "I *need* you, E. You have to help me. I *need* this."

"I know you do, honey." He really did. "But we can't. We have to get Julio and get out of here before they drive the Guardians off." As good as the Guardians were, they could level the place, but wouldn't be able to reach Madame G.

"Just a quickie, E, so I can concentrate."

He batted her hands away again, and grasped her by the shoulders, giving her a little shake. "The feeling won't go away, only time will make it go away. I'm not debasing you like that, and I'm not putting your rescue and Julio's rescue on the line for a quick fuck. Not even for you."

Blinking and shaking her head like she was trying to clear her mind, he knew he was getting through to her. But the drugs pumped her hormones higher and higher until they overrode her common sense so she would jump on the nearest dick available.

Or the drugs tried to because she had fended off the recruit pretty well, but E's presence made her throw her sense out the window. The pheromones she exuded would harden any male who came near her.

"Let's get you some clothes, get me some weapons, and go meet Julio."

He rummaged around the drawers in the room, looking for a gown or shirt, something to cover his mate's delectable body. If the situation wasn't so dire, he didn't know if he could steel himself against the scents she was throwing off and ignore her nudity.

While he was bent over, opening the drawers that lined the walls, she came up behind him, rubbing his back, pressing into his backside. E bit his cheek and cursed mentally. She wasn't going to make this easy; she couldn't help herself.

Gritting his teeth to ignore his own jacked-up libido, he finally found a drawer with cloth of some sort. A hospital robe. Perfect.

He spun on the woman pawing him from behind and swung the robe around her shoulders. When he snagged one arm to help her into it, she shook him off to keep trying for his pants.

Should he give in? Just a quickie?

No. Nope. Once he went there, he'd have as hard a time stopping as Ana. He had to remember his son was waiting for them, and he needed get his sex-crazed mate to safety.

E wrestled her into the robe, got it tied around her roaming arms, and dragged her to the door. He'd feel a lot better if he had a weapon, or twenty. Especially dragging a horned up female down the hall. The primary armory was on the main level, but they had some storage lockers in the lower levels, usually to hold the weapons they stripped off their captives.

He'd have to take the long way before meeting X at the stairwell, but he couldn't fight his way out and protect his family with his bare hands.

"E, please," Ana pleaded. "It's starting to hurt."

"I can't change that Ana. We need to keep going."

He made the mistake of looking back at her, which he'd been avoiding because she was as gorgeous as she always had been, and was exceedingly turned on. And he was trying to be a good boy and keep his hands to himself, but the tears running down her cheeks were almost too much.

He tore his gaze away from her and gripped her hand harder as he pulled her along, speeding toward a storage locker he really hoped wasn't empty.

They reached the room that might hold some weapons, and if his luck was still holding out, ammo. He used the mad doctor's finger to gain access. Pulling Ana inside, he didn't bother turning on the light. It could bring unwanted attention, and he could make do with his keen vision.

E was rewarded with handguns, knives, even a sword inside the locker. E rushed to strap some knives to his legs and stuffed a couple of guns into his waistband, pocketing as many bullet-filled magazines as he could.

Stiffening as a scent assaulted his nose, he whipped his head up, dreading what he was going to see when he turned toward Ana.

Sure enough, she was leaning against a wall, palming herself and grinding into her hand. Her robe hitched up in the front, one long, curvy leg exposed.

Aw, hell. In any other instance, that'd be some erotic shit. For now, he'd file it away as, *Can you totally do that in front of me later?* and try to get to her to stop.

Or better yet, he could strap some weapons onto her body while her hands were occupied.

Only one knife was left that was in a case he could strap onto her, and one gun with a full clip in it, but no other ammo. Better than nothing.

Walking up to her, staring at the wall above her head as she bit her lip and moaned, he strapped the knife to her upper arm instead of getting close to ground zero. He couldn't risk accidentally fondling his mate and not being able to stop once his hands landed on her scrumptious thighs.

As soon as he touched her upper arm, her eyes flew open and focused on him. Her breath was erratic and hitched, she was nearing a climax. Making quick work of the knife strap around her arm, she reached for him with her free hand, twisting it in his shirt. He stood frozen while her eyes rolled back before she squeezed them tight and shuttered out her orgasm, slumping against the wall with her aftershocks.

Shiiiiiit…That was hot. And completely inappropriate for him to think so. Grabbing her by the shoulders, he raised her back to fully standing. "We need to get going."

Her head rested against the wall, moving back and forth. Ana swallowed hard. "I can't go. It's building again. I thought that would help, but it's like it made it worse."

"That's how those drugs work. They keep you going until you're completely used and destroyed inside."

Tears shimmered in her eyes. "You went through this?"

"I was mindless coming out of my conversion, a slave to my base needs and my body only thought it had one need. But yes, you're experiencing something similar."

"I'm so sorry," she whispered.

Taken aback, he couldn't imagine what she had to be sorry for but there was no time to find out.

Pulling her along back into the hallway, she kept muttering "sorry" over and over again. A familiar scent tickled his nose again and he felt Ana stumble behind him. Hell no, she couldn't be stroking one off again.

"I'm so sorry," she sobbed. "I've only experienced a fraction of what you went through, and now I'm preventing you from escaping and helping our son."

E had never seen Ana so distraught. During their marriage, while they had financial stress and work concerns, she'd been his rock. And since her fiancé had turned on her and tried to kill and then kidnap her son, she had retained her calm. Then he appeared in front of her, her dead husband come alive, and she was thrown into a supernatural world. But it wasn't until now, when she thought she was failing him and risking their son's life that she was crumbling, a burden because of the drugs they pumped into her.

"Come here." He pulled her closer, letting her keep her hand over her center because she couldn't help herself.

She tumbled into him, her body seeking his, urging him to give her some relief. Instead, he centered his hand over that sweet spot in her neck that, with just enough pressure, would grant her the gift of unconsciousness. Her body so starved for touch, she pressed into his hand, a brief flare of surprise crossed her face before oblivion took her.

Refusing to feel even a little guilt, he bent down to swing her up over his shoulder. E made his way to the spot where he was counting on X to be with Julio.

*****

Agent J scanned X's leather-clad body, lingering on the juncture of her thighs. "Meet me in five minutes, Agent X. I've gotta throw some food at this kid, and then we can," his eyes drifted up from her breasts, lifted high from the black corset she wore, "get down to business."

Putting her hands on her hips, she threw her shoulders back to jut her lifted breasts out further. "Don't keep me waiting, J-man. I don't have all fucking day."

"You worried those Guardians will breach the walls? Shouldn't you be up there defending the place?" So far, the shifters had been attacking the walls with what X would guess was rocket-propelled grenades. Madame G's supernatural defenses were holding firmly in place. And would until X gave them the signal to boost and concentrate their power so E and his family could get out of there.

"I will after a good lay." With that, she spun and sauntered out, knowing she had the male's full attention.

She crossed the hall into Agent J's office, sat in his chair, and threw her feet up on the desk with her hands hooked behind her head. No use getting undressed until she had to. Besides, she could always use it as a show to distract the Agent.

Reflecting on the excuses she told J for being there, she mused how different they were from her real intentions. "E's been gone too long," she had whined to Agent J. "I need some attention."

The door across the hall slammed shut. A heartbeat passed before Agent J strode into his office. An uneasy feeling settled deep into her belly when she saw the manacles dangling from his hand.

She maintained a cool expression on her face, swung her legs down and stood, casually untying the leather threads of her corset. Agent J's eyes hooked on her hands, momentarily mesmerized.

Males. A few scraps of leather and lace and they lost all focus.

X shed the corset and worked her wispy undershirt shirt out of her pants, showing him a hint of skin. She lowered her voice to a sultry purr. "Have a seat."

He tossed the silver cuffs onto his desk and leaned over, licking his bottom lip while he watched her show. "I have a better idea. You slide those tight pants down and have a seat."

Hmmm, no. She didn't plan on getting that far with the Agent before he lost his head, and not the one all his blood was rushing to.

She eyed him coyly, dropping the shirt back over her toned stomach, she slowly worked on the fastenings of her pants. "What do you have planned?"

He gave her a fang-filled grin. "You strike me as the bondage type, X. Let's have a little fun."

Fuck. No. She ditched the act, her rescue plan would be carried out the hard way. She zipped her pants back up with a sigh and tucked her shirt in. "Sex with you is far from fun, J-wad."

The male's face clouded over. "Do you think I'm an idiot, X? You came sniffing around when your partner was in deep shit, and now you're back when I have his son."

She studied her fingernails and shrugged nonchalantly. "Busted. I want to see the little guy E left me for."

"Bullshit. You're too weak to stomach what we do to children. I can't believe Madame G keeps you around." Drawing a long, sinister blade, preparing for battle, his arrogance kept him talking. "You're too late," he sneered. "The little brat got his injections. He transitioned faster than anyone we've ever seen. I think we might breed his mama, build our own Agent army." Laughing at the innocent's demise, he attempted to enrage X even further. "I think I'll have a go at her a few times, too. She'll be more memorable than you."

X could only smirk at him, wishing she could inform him why she was somewhat forgettable, though she usually overrode her hypnotism with a few planted memories of what a magnificent lay she was.

"You and me, then? Wanna place any bets?" Withdrawing her favorite fighting blade, she crouched into a combative stance, circling the desk with J doing the same.

"No need. I'm going to play with you a little before I kill you."

"Aww," she cooed, blowing him a kiss, "you say the sweetest things."

Rather than jumping the desk and attacking like he'd expect, she waited until she had circled to one of the narrow ends and shoved. Her move took him by surprise, but instead of the heavy wood desk trapping him against the wall, he flashed out.

Tensing, X prepared herself. Once she saw a hint of movement, she pivoted and slashed with her blade. Satisfaction poured through her at his grunt of pain, but she narrowly missed his arm whipping out to gut her. He flashed again.

Gah! She hated fighting vampires. Only the biggest cowards flashed repeatedly instead of facing a fight until the job got done. Agent J was big cock on campus when his prey was locked in a room or strapped to a table, yet here he was flashing constantly, thinking it gave him the advantage.

A flash to her right had her spinning only to see J disappear again. Dammit. Before she could pivot back around, he was aiming for her between the ribs.

Air whooshed out as heat seared through the stab wound. He withdrew the blade to strike at her throat. Reaching out, she grabbed onto him in case he tried to flash again and jerked him toward her so she could jack her knee up into his groin.

Bull's-eye! He snarled in pain and rage, and flashed. She was hanging onto him so he took her with him. A non-vampire would have a severe case of vertigo after flashing, and clearly J was gambling on that. X didn't want to let him down.

She gasped, pretending to swoon once they appeared at the other end of the office and he bared his fangs in wicked glee thinking he had her.

She used his hubris and their close proximity to shove her blade into his belly and yank down. He snarled and stabbed at her, but the pain was staggering and slowed his defenses. X easily batted his armed hand away, jerked her knife out, and flashed behind him.

The Agent doubled over, his gaze darting around, because the last thing he expected was for the notorious shifter Agent to be able to flash like a vampire. Yanking his head up by his dark hair, she drew her knife deep across the front of his throat.

Agent J dropped to his knees, weakened from the blood loss, and X traded her smaller knife for his larger one, making quick work of removing the male's head from his body. Yeah, cowards might flash during a fight, but she was a female with a deadline and a kid to rescue.

The stab wound between her ribs throbbed, making each breath a shade shy of excruciating, but she bundled up the pain and shoved it into the dark recesses of her mind where every other unsavory experience was sent. Next, she looked at her bloodied, gory hands. Maybe a good washing before barging in on Julio, claiming to rescue him, would be in order.

The attached bathroom in J's office had enough soap to scrub as much blood off her hands as possible, along with a small hand towel to stuff in her shirt over her seeping wound. Lacing the corset back over it would hold it in place until her body took care of the healing and sealed the wound. Looking up, she caught her reflection in the mirror and went still.

Her hair was a mess; E's rescue and her battle with J having mussed it up more than a little. She'd have to use more gel in it next time. The brilliant green eyes she inherited from her shifter father were ironically gleaming from her vampire heritage.

She looked at her reflection in the mirror every day, why pause now?

Because for the first time, she could look at herself with something other than forced indifference. Indifference to her actions of the day, or of the duties she would be leaving to perform. Indifference to her situation, and refusing to compare the female she saw now, to the one she used to see before tragedy had struck twelve years ago. She had been the innocent, all-American teenager, who played volleyball, volunteered during the summer, and walked dogs for The Humane Society.

So what did she see now? A badass hybrid who had crawled back from the grave and was ready to carry out her destiny, hopefully before Madame G severely punished her for her bold transgression. X was confident Madame G wouldn't kill her, not her stolen prize—a shifter. But the punishment would be staggeringly severe, prolonged, and absolutely worth it. Running her fingers through her hair, fluffing the top back into place, she took one last look and went to find Julio.

Chapter Fourteen

Hanging out in the stairwell at Sigma's compound, cradling an unconscious Ana, was not a fun time. Faint moans and wails echoed on the subtle breeze that flowed through the concrete walls. No one, not even the most hardened or jaded recruits, or Agents, used the stairs. Surveillance had been setup on their entrances after Dani and Mercury each used them in their own escapes. E knew that regardless, they weren't monitored very well. The recruits on security detail told tales of being too creeped out by shadows that ebbed and flowed in the steady light, along with indistinct faces with gaping jaws, to watch the footage even a little.

E couldn't deny the tickles he felt along his spine standing just inside the door of the second level below ground. It was like the spirits, if they were real, were fascinated by a living, breathing body in their territory. After his talk with Ana, and their conjectures of Madame G's power source, he was starting to believe the spirits existed, hoped they despised the dark madam as much as he did.

After all, Dani and Mercury used the stairwell to get to safety with no incident.

Readjusting Ana, he looked over her face for the millionth time. She was still passed out and he worried she shouldn't be. His choke-out should've only lasted a few minutes at most. Maybe it had only been a few minutes, but every second of the escape attempt felt like an eternity. He scanned his mate's slack features, concerned there was a gray tint to her color that wasn't there before. Though her chest rose and fell rhythmically, the movements lacked the robust flow of when he'd watch her sleep.

A soft rap on the door had him bringing his aim up to above the door handle. When the door swung open, E recognized X's gun enter just before her she poked her head in.

"Dude, it's creepy in here," she said.

She gently nudged Julio in. E wanted to drop to his knees and wrap up his son into a bear hug.

Instead the boy's face lit up. "Dad!" He clutched E around the waist, who awkwardly rubbed his son's back, still holding Ana with one arm and his gun in the other.

X stepped all the way in, softly closing the door behind her. He had the urge to tell her he could take over from there, but he wasn't a raging moron. He had a kid and an unconscious adult, with weapons that weren't his tucked in random places all over his body. The compound was under attack, and all

Agents and recruits would be defending the first level.

X jutted her chin toward Ana being hauled back up to his shoulder to advance up the stairs. Her gesture silently asked if Ana was okay.

"Dunno," he muttered so Julio couldn't hear.

"Why? What's wrong with Mom?" Julio caught the unspoken question and inaudible answer regardless. E finally had a good look at his boy.

Where his son had been a tall kid before, he looked like he'd grown an inch or two and put on five to ten pounds of muscle since E'd last seen him. The innocence was still there, but dulled, becoming overwritten with a worldly knowledge that things weren't all as they seemed. A sharp inhale confirmed E's suspicion. They'd altered his son; made him more like his daddy than ever before, and that made E feel like he failed his child.

Clapping E on the back, urging him to go ahead of her, all X said was, "Maybe it's for the best."

He passed her an incredulous look before making his way up the next two levels. Transforming his son to become their personal monster was *for the best*?

"Don't look at me like that, Biggie. It's not like you're leaving here and going to the 'burbs to drive a minivan and coach little league." X kept Julio between them while she covered them from behind. "Now the playing field's been leveled, and Julio can be ready for the game of life as you now know it."

Terribly true. E hadn't given much thought to where they would run to if they managed to get out of the building and away from Sigma. It sure wouldn't be to go house hunting and check out local schools. There'd always be a bolo on all three of them from Sigma. The shifter and vampire communities would have avid interests in obtaining them. Not only for their knowledge of Sigma but because they couldn't allow another supernatural species to roam without govern. If they allowed them to remain alive at all.

Reaching the first level, the walls shook more with each hit the Guardians lobbed at the compound. E could hear yelling and return gunfire from the rooms facing the trees. Turning back to X, he awaited her instructions.

Before she could speak, a rapid series of explosions pounded the north wall.

"That's our cue. Head toward the noise. Those blasts should have weakened the walls so you can finish blowing your way out from the inside."

E gave his partner a calculating look. She knew to begin their escape with the first bomb, but after that, either their timing during the siege was a happy coincidence or she was communicating with them.

"You know, I forget you don't need an excellent cell phone carrier." She had tried several times to see if E could develop telepathy, or be able to communicate mentally with just her, but it always failed. He often didn't think of how she could talk mentally to any shifter within proximity.

She shot him a cocky smirk. "Never forget how phenomenal I am."

E went to open the door, but waited until two Agents rushed by, fleeing an explosion in the north wing. Taking advantage of the extra time, he checked on Ana. Her color had faded even more and her breathing was growing erratic. He almost swore, but remembered Julio's acute hearing.

"Go," X urged. "I'll watch your ass until you get out of the walls. Then keep anyone from getting a good shot at you."

"Come with us, X. It's too dangerous for you to stay." And he couldn't leave her. They'd been inseparable for nearly a decade, and although he gained the two most important people in his life, he didn't know what he'd do without the indomitable Agent X. She'd become his only friend, his family.

"No can do, Biggie. My work here is not done." When he opened his mouth to argue, she gave her head a curt shake. "I can't roam this earth knowing that vampire hag is terrorizing innocent people. I can still find a way."

Explosions rocked the walls, Agents shouted, and his mate's health was declining. Even the maybe-spirits of the stairwell seemed agitated at his delay.

E pulled the door open as quietly as possible. Not sensing any immediate danger, X went out first and waved E and Julio to follow. Together, they hugged the wall with Julio in the middle and made their way down a corridor, heading to where the worst damage to the exterior walls had been done.

"Behind you!" Julio spun around to tug on his shirt, craning his neck to look behind E.

E twisted, gun raised. Two recruits darted out of an office the trio had just passed, preparing to attack the small group. E quickly took them down, each with a head shot, before they could aim and fire.

Julio saw everything, and it killed E inside that his son had to witness the violence, that this was his world now.

"What's wrong with Mom?" Julio asked as they continued to rush toward where the explosions had been centered moments before. "She doesn't smell right."

Hell. E knew something was wrong with Ana, but now Julio claimed her scent was off and that was bad. Just bad. No matter the species, dying changed a person, altered their biochemistry, especially if it was prolonged at any rate. Not only did Ana look sickly, she smelled sickly and he had no idea why.

Talking to Julio, knowing X would get the hint, E reassured him. "Maybe by the time we get out of here, Doc will have been notified to be ready to help your mom."

X threw him a sardonic look over her shoulder. "Subtle, Biggie, subtle."

"What's that word mean?" Julio asked her.

"Look it up in the dictionary," she threw back at him.

Julio made a sound of frustration. "You sound like Mom. I'll just Google it."

E's lips quirked, grateful Julio was distracted from Ana's dire situation.

"There's your exit." X stepped over the shrapnel left behind from a heavy metal door. No other Agents had come to defend the breach of perimeter and that served E's escape plans just fine. Climbing out of the shattered concrete walls would be the easy part. Getting himself, the precious package he cradled, and his beloved son across the span of lawn to the protection of the trees would be a harrowing experience. He was fast, his son was probably just as fast now, but several Agents and recruits were shooting out of windows into the very tree line he needed to make it to.

"Nice." X cleared the room, stepping carefully over debris, making sure to stay away from the already gaping hole in the wall. E helped Julio over the wreckage of the door and into the room before he gingerly stepped inside.

Once they were in, X fell back into the hallway. He heard movement down the corridor.

"Get to the garages," she commanded whomever must've been heading their way "we don't have enough coverage there."

E waited, preparing to jump out and help X if need be, but they listened to her, changing course to head to the garages. She wasn't lying exactly.

Leaving in a car would hinder more than help; the trees would be his best chance at rescuing his family. Several Agents and recruits had cars, and they could easily chase them with wheels, but in the trees, many Sigma personnel were out of their comfort zone and couldn't congregate in groups as easily as they could on the road. So no, the garages weren't targeted as much by the Guardians.

He gave one final nod to his partner, the female who had been his savior. She saved him from himself and then from others on countless missions, eventually allowing him to get back to his family.

"See you later." It was all he could say, because telling her good-bye was too hard.

Her vivid green eyes said she didn't believe that would happen. She committed her entirety to their final goal. "Go get your creep on, Biggie." Her reply was what she always said when he was leaving to spy on his family.

Scanning the yawning hole with daylight pouring through, E realized…it was fucking daylight. He'd been knocked out so long, he'd forgotten the time of day. Of course the Guardians would attack early in the day. Send their message to leave their territory the hell alone and limit the vampires' retaliation. Daylight secured the vampires to the compound, and boy, would they be pissed.

Feeling more optimistic than he had all night, or day, he pulled Julio over blasted fragments of concrete to the side of the opening so he could peer out.

The stretch of lawn was clear. Of people anyway. It was covered with dirt chunks and hunks of sod that had been blown out by bombs that didn't make it to the compound. Glass and cement debris stretched from the exterior of the wall.

E looked down. He was still wearing his boots, but Julio was only in a T-shirt and jeans, with bare feet poking out the bottom. "I'm going to jump down with you. It's not far, but there's glass so I need to carry you past it." *And block you with my body*, but E left that part out.

Julio's wide, brown eyes held a solid dose of fear along with a dash of excitement. He looked like he wanted to argue that he could do it himself, then he glanced at where Ana was still cradled over E's shoulder.

"We need to get her help. She won't last much longer."

E absolutely agreed. "Let's go." Holstering his gun, which meant sliding it back into his waistband, he secured Ana better on his shoulder, worried at the amount of her body that would be targeted. But he needed to lift Julio and shield him as much as possible, too, and that left little room for Ana.

Picking up his boy, Julio wrapped his arms around E's shoulder and his mother's legs to hold on. E ducked and leaped through the opening, barely clearing both his feet and head of becoming snagged in the jagged stone jutting out, and landed solidly. He spun out, increasing his speed as much as he could, as quickly as he could.

Someone shouted from one of the windows, and E could feel the weapons re-sighting onto his back and Ana's head. They would be shooting to kill.

A deafening sound thundered at the edge of the trees, like a pack of lions roared and heading his way. Dust and debris kicked up by a wall of wind right in front of E as he ran. He braced himself, ready to spin and protect his son so he could still breathe through the dirt, but to his astonishment, the wall parted around them to clatter and heave its load into any open windows.

"Dad, put me down. I can run." Julio let go of his hold on him and squirmed to wiggle down.

"Stop. I'm gonna drop you." With the aid of whichever Guardian had the power to harness the wind, they were nearly to the tree line. Stray shots tossed up bits of dirt and grass at his feet, but no one was able to get a good zero in on them with the earth blowing straight into their faces.

Julio persisted until E was forced to set him down in front of him, otherwise he'd drop Ana, too. E slowed to cover Julio with his body, but he didn't slow long. Soon his son was a blur and made it to the trees, while E still had a hundred yards to cover with his mate bouncing on his shoulder.

"Julio! Get behind a tree and wait for me." E raced after his son. Did Julio know he could do that?

Rushing to the cover of the trees, E let his senses flare out. How many Agents and recruits had made it to the woods to hunt down the shifters?

Movement to his left had him grabbing for his gun and aiming at the shadow. A flash of familiar braided coppery hair stalled him from shooting. Kaitlyn had come to help. She stepped around the tree she'd been using for cover, holding a metal tube perched on her shoulder and wearing an odd-looking bandolier containing nothing but empty holders. The acrid smell of gunpowder clouding her body and her wicked grin suggested she was the main grenade launcher.

"Let's head down to the highway. The commander said we need to get Ana to Doc ASAP. He's waiting for her and Julio."

Thank you, X. E would forever be indebted to the female, to all of the Guardians. "Julio, stay with Kaitlyn, no matter how fast you can run now."

"Come on, kid. I'll set the pace. I can't have you smacking into any trees with your new horsepower."

Julio's face screwed up. "Horsepower?"

"Yeah, like a car engine." At Julio's blank look, she just shook her head. "Later, kid. You'll thoroughly learn about cars later."

E gently brought Ana down to cradle her in front him, knowing she had already endured a good shaking when he jumped out onto the lawn and ran across it. Her chest barely rose.

"We need to move."

Kaitlyn glanced back at E, hearing the contained panic in his voice, then looked at Ana's face. Her nostrils flared, like she too could smell his mate was nearing her end. Heading deeper into the trees, dodging branches, she continually picked up her pace until she found a swift speed Julio could keep up with and still watch his footing.

Random gunshots popped through the trees, growing fainter as they ran. The terrain wasn't as rugged in this part of the woods, across the river from where the Guardians resided. Hills gently rolled, and while the brush was thicker, it wasn't impossible to get through. Noisy, but doable.

E scanned around him as much as possible without knocking himself, or Ana, into any trunks or limbs, worried about the clamor they were making in their haste. With good reason. He sensed two Agents quickly closing in.

Kaitlyn did, too. "Keep going. They'll get dealt with."

He hugged Ana closer and sped up in accordance with Kaitlyn's burst of speed.

From behind him, a shout and gunfire, and a bullet going far to the right of where they ran. Wolf, E sensed. One of Guardians was in their shifter form hunting Agents.

Three sharp bursts of gunfire were followed by snarling and growling. The second Agent who had been pursuing them was now a non-issue. He'd heal, but E hoped the shifter didn't get shot for his efforts.

The highway was coming up quickly. Two dark SUVs parked in the tree line, neatly camouflaged from passing cars. They closed in on them and it wouldn't be too soon.

"Kaitlyn, can you take Julio in one vehicle while one of the wolves behind us drives me and Ana?"

One look at the alarm written on E's face and she hauled up Julio, opening the backdoor and buckling him in. E beelined for the backseat of the second SUV, not wanting Julio to see what he had to do next. Spreading Ana across the backseat, he wrestled his body in-between the seats. Using those life-saving skills he had learned years ago, but certainly hadn't used lately, he tilted her head back and leaned down to breathe for her while trying to capture a pulse.

The door opened and he sensed a Guardian slide into the driver's seat, the sound of bare skin on vinyl. Mercury. The male had shifted and climbed in without dressing first, aware of the dire situation for Ana. Without a word, the Guardian fired up the engine and pulled onto the road, steadily increasing speed until they were flying down the highway.

E continued breathing for Ana, her pulse thready, but present. He was her lungs, her life force, to keep her heart trudging along until she was strong enough to stay alive on her own.

Eternity came and went in the drive to the Guardians' headquarters. The SUV pulled to a stop and the door opened on E's side. E finally brought his attention off his wife and looked up to see the tall, lanky doctor with a somber expression.

"I have everything ready, Agent." Doc squatted down, tilting Ana's head back as far as he could on the seat. He gently pried Ana's mouth open and maneuvered a long, slightly curved tube into her airway. Once it was secured in place, he strapped a mask over Ana's slack mouth, the clear hosing running to an oxygen tank on the cot he had ready for the unconscious woman.

E helped lift Ana and hand her out to the doctor. Once he was out of the vehicle, it was a case of anxiously standing around while Doc strapped his mate to various medical sensors anchored to the cot. E was too wound up to even pace. His mate was knocking at death's door, and he could do nothing about it. He didn't even know *why* she was in the condition she was in. Mercury had donned a pair of shorts, waiting patiently alongside E, who was grateful the male wasn't a chatty fucker, trying to take his mind off his dying mate and the son he'd have to tell.

"Do you know anything of what they gave her?" the doctor asked, sticking differently colored stickers all over Ana's bare chest. To each sticker, he hooked a different wire that led to a monitor. Once all the wires were attached, wavy lines appeared on the monitor and E remembered enough from his cop days when he got radioed to assist with medical emergencies, that the lines weren't nearly spiked enough, nor as rhythmic as they should be.

"I've got no clue," E said gruffly. He should've found someone to torture to get that information before they left. But who and with what extra time? "X said they planned to enhance her, but with what, I don't know. Then they loaded her with Sigma's version of a mega-roofie."

Doc motioned to Mercury to push the cot as he rushed alongside, checking all of her vitals. "When did she lose consciousness?"

"I…" guilt poured through him, "I made her pass out because she was in so much pain with the drugs they gave her. I couldn't rescue her in that condition; she could barely walk." He said it more to justify it to himself than to the others present.

To the doctor's credit, he only bobbed his head in confirmation, but gave E no signs of recrimination for his actions. The group sped to the rooms Doc had setup as his own little treatment center, and Mercury pushed the cot into what resembled a real ER room.

Once inside, the wiry shifter stood back, facing Ana's prone form, his hand on his chin propped up by his other arm. E wanted to shout "What the hell, dude?" but forced himself to wait patiently. Mercury even aimed a perplexed look at the doctor but remained silent. E had a feeling he stayed to protect the doctor from any bad news he might have to deliver to E.

"Agent E," Doc began, rubbing his chin, "I have a theory, but that's all. I can find nothing medically wrong, other than she's fading and we're keeping her from completing the process of shutting her body down." He went over to a floor-to-ceiling cupboard in the corner and gathered supplies: a large syringe and needle and...Band-Aids? "From what I know of how Sigma alters their Agents and how mating works, I suspect her body's at war with itself."

"Whaddya mean?"

The doctor gestured to a chair in the corner. "Have a seat and I'll tell you. I need to take some blood."

E promptly followed directions, flopping down in the chair, mollified that they were doing something that would help his mate, the love of his life.

"When you mated her, it worked like Dani and Mercury's mating. Their bond overrode the blood bond Madame G requires of her recruits. It's more natural, runs deeper." Doc yanked up E's sleeve and palpated a vein, needing no tourniquet. "In Ana's case, the process was reversed. She mated you first and then Madame G tried to bond with her. I suspect it was too soon. Ana's body hadn't had time to solidify your bond. Kaitlyn said her natural abilities were developing stronger, sharper...so I could be wrong."

"And if you are?" E watched numbly as the male cleaned off his inner elbow with an alcohol swab, wishing the cool sensation would wash the fear from his body.

Ripping a thick needle out of its packaging, he twisted it onto the barrel of a syringe and deftly stabbed it into E's arm. "This shouldn't hurt her regardless. But she's been held prisoner, no doubt not fed well. She needs to heal *and* fight off Madame G's serum. Your blood should aid that process and maybe, well, I hope also give your bond to her a boost."

Deep red blood filled the syringe until the doctor couldn't pull the plunger back any further. Then he withdrew, pushing a piece of gauze onto the entry point. He folded E's arm up to hold it in place and tossed the Band-Aid to him. Turning to Ana and lifting her sleeve, he wrapped his large hand around her delicate upper arm as a makeshift tourniquet and inserted the very same needle, slowly depressing the plunger until all of E's blood was emptied into his mate.

After withdrawing the needle and slapping a bandage on Ana, he tossed the empty syringe into a large red bucket and got his stethoscope ready to listen to Ana's chest.

E shot up from his seat at a strangled sound coming from his mate's gurney. Ana's eyes flew open, her mouth open in a silent scream. Her back arched up and the scream broke free, echoing through the room.

"Ana!" E leapt to her side, shoving Doc out of the way. He held onto her shoulders so she wouldn't shake herself off the cot. "Ana!" He searched for the doctor, finding him approaching warily, brushing off his white coat after hitting the wall when E shoved him. "What's happening?"

Ana flailed from side to side, strangled screams bounced off the walls, her legs scissoring.

"Agent E," Doc said cautiously, holding his hand out like it was going to placate the crazed Agent. "I need to monitor her."

E snarled at him. In his mind, all he heard was them telling him to get away from his mate. She might be in her death throes; he wasn't leaving her side. Mercury grabbed his shoulders to move him away so Doc could get in to monitor Ana, but E exploded. Throwing elbows back, kicking behind him, E struggled to shake the burly male. Leave him the hell alone to protect Ana's beautiful body as she writhed in pain.

Mercury's thick arms wrapped around him in a bear hug, damn near lifting him off the ground. E flung his head back, butting Mercury in the nose, righteously satisfied when he heard the sharp crack of bone.

Expecting Mercury to howl in pain, throw him down, and jump on him, E wasn't prepared for the stabbing sensation in his upper arm. Energy drained out of his movements as Doc removed an empty syringe. Shit.

His head lolled back onto Mercury's shoulder and rolled to the side as he strained to keep his thrashing mate within view. The doctor had already turned from him, concentrating on the woman in pain, who was still screaming in a now hoarse voice.

"We'll take care of her." Mercury repeated in E's ear as blackness won the battle and claimed its victory.

Chapter Fifteen

Elephants. It must've been an elephant stampede and Ana got caught in it. In fact, one might have even stopped and done the samba on her body. Which one of those gray fuckers poured acid down her throat? It burned like embers still smoldered in her tonsils.

Ana blinked her eyes open. The room was blessedly dim. Were her ears muted or was the room really was that quiet? She squinted and peered around, seeing the room she was in for the first time. A hospital?

"Mrs. Esposito?" a deep voice addressed her.

Who called her that anymore? She went by Ms. if at all possible. People assumed with that title that she was either divorced, widowed, or a righteous feminist and never made personal inquiries. It only took a few awkward conversations before she chucked the Mrs. out the window.

She slid her gaze toward the voice because turning her head made the drums within it beat harder. He was a familiar tall, lean male. From his scent, he was a shifter, and, oh yes, the pseudo-doctor who worked for the Guardians.

With that last thought, all of her memories came flooding back—her fiancé's plan to hurt her, her dead husband she was now mated to, Sigma's capture, and…oh. That last memory would have been damn near embarrassing if the situation hadn't been so critical and she hadn't been in so much pain.

"Julio? E?" She croaked through her scratchy, parched throat.

The male gave a small reassuring smile, laced with a trace of guilt. "Julio is playing with Sarah's dog, Apollo. Your mate is resting. You were having complications from your treatment and he got upset. We had to sedate him." She didn't miss the change in his expression. Yep, it was guilt. "Unfortunately, my doses are pre-measured for shifter males and Agent E is not exactly one. So it knocked him out for longer than expected."

"I imagine his biochemistry is still a bit more human when it comes to drug interactions. The shifter and vampire traits his DNA has incorporated, can tolerate the dosage and heal any overdosing, but cannot metabolize them differently otherwise." Maybe she should be alarmed, but talking drug interactions was actually the most normal thing that had happened to her in weeks.

Appearing extremely pleased, Doc gave her another small smile. "My thoughts exactly and I would love to look into it more with you. I haven't had time to conduct much research, I'm still building my lab. With blood samples from you,

Agent E, and only with your consent, little Julio, I would love to gain further understanding into what Sigma has developed for enhancing their Agents."

"That. Would be. Fascinating!" Her pounding head and body aches forgotten, Ana's excitement overrode them both. "Like, how much is supernatural and how much is chemistry? It can't be as simple as, I put my blood in yours. Otherwise there would have been human conversion accidents as long as there's been vampires and shifters." Ana tried to sit up, captivated by the topic, when she winced at the sharp pain in her ribs. Examining herself for the first time, she saw she was wearing nothing but the robe E had thrown around her. Thankfully it was tied shut, with wires attached to stickers hooked on her chest and winding out from inside the closure. "What did you mean by treatment?"

"I think you're on the mend, but of course I'd like to study your blood work in greater detail." Ana nodded absently at his inferred request. "After Agent E knocked you out so he could rescue you," *He did what?* "your body continued to fight itself over the Agent's bond and the cocktail Sigma gave you. And while under the influence of the sex drugs they administered, it was too much too soon. On a hunch, we injected another dose of your mate's blood, hoping it would strengthen the bond that was already there."

Ana blew out a gusty breath. She almost died and hadn't a clue. "So did it?"

"I can only assume yes, but it was quite an internal struggle." The male gave a rueful shake of his head. "At times, quite an external struggle for us."

Thus the reason she was so stinking sore. She reached out and grabbed the doctor's hand, causing him to nearly jump out of his skin. "Thank you, Garreth. Can I go see my family now?"

*****

E felt like he had to use a pry bar to get his eyelids to open, but the intoxicating scent wafting over him roused more than just his consciousness. Once they focused, he was greeted with an image that must have been from his dreams.

"You don't know how many times when you were a cop that I worried about this happening, me standing over your hospital bed. But," Ana leaned back, looking at how he was stretched out over the white blanket, left to sleep off his sedation, "it's much better than standing beside your casket."

Instead of sitting up, because he was still too lethargic, he pulled her down on top of him. His delightful mate spread herself over him, her borrowed pajama pants and top pressed to his grungy clothes.

Kissing her was heaven, as close as he was ever going to get, as close as he needed to be. She melted into him, cradling his face with her soft hands as her legs straddled his body.

Releasing her mouth briefly, he asked, "You okay?" Of course she was, she was here. It was the dude in him, he had to ask.

"Yeah. I just checked on Julio and he's in little boy heaven. Right now he's deep into *Mario Kart*, racing Ronnie. And," she rocked her pelvis into him, rubbing the already straining erection that had come awake as soon as he had, "I think the good doctor knows we might be in here a while, because he said he was going to the kitchen to eat, and then go for a long run."

Hell. Yes.

Wait. "Are the drugs still affecting you?"

She whispered into his ear. "Would it matter if they were?" Reaching between them, she undid his pants and palmed his throbbing shaft.

"Yes? No? Fuck it." He ripped her pajama bottoms off, positioned her over him, and slammed inside.

Ana barely had time to gasp before he brought her lips back down to his and thrust urgently until they were both crying their finish within seconds.

Her hands still fisted into his shirt from her release, she swayed gently coming down from the wave of climax. "I guess we both needed that."

"I need you."

A sweet smile spread across Ana's kiss-swollen lips. "I love you. Have I told you that lately?"

Words he'd die again to hear. E broke out in a triumphant grin. "Hell, baby. I never quit loving you. But to hear you say that me, to Agent E, is beyond my wildest dreams."

Ana pulled her top off and granted E the sweet, sweet view of her naked breasts, tipped with those lovely cinnamon nipples that made his mouth water. "Now let me show you."

*****

X assumed the dutiful position knowing a world of pain was heading her way. She was in Madame G's elegant suite, but her dark master had not yet appeared.

A yelp perked X ears and she chanced looking up, intending to throw her eyes right back to the floor after a little looky-look. Instead, from a hidden door in the office chamber, Madame G dragged a female out by her long, pale hair.

The seer.

Risking the view since torture was sure to follow anyway, X scanned the female sliding on her butt, her feet scrambling to gain purchase, with the madam's fist twisted in her scalp. Distraught, confused eyes of the palest turquoise flashed up, confirming X's suspicions this was a shifter who was gifted, or in her case cursed, with visions. X had been taught as a child that seers often lacked pigment and tended to be light of hair, skin, and eye color, some kind of genetic anomaly to alert shifters to the gifted young so they could be properly handled and trained. It did no population good to have premonitions spewed indiscriminately.

Only recently had X been clued in to the possibility that Madame G's foreknowledge was not innate, but stolen from another species. Shifter seers were heavily protected by the shifter council. It was no wonder Madame G kept her prize hidden. If they found out, not only would the council continually attempt rescue, but it gave her the added bonus of perceived omnipotence.

How in the world had the madam bagged herself a seer?

X dropped her gaze back into place, conveying the proper amount of respect in her mistress' presence. Any little way to boost her standing could only help her after she had helped E bust out his family. She was pretty sure she wouldn't be killed over it. Not completely confident, but whatever. Her odds usually sucked anyway, and allowing E to be systematically destroyed as his family was manipulated and mutated was not worth her life. Their value far outranked hers. So she risked a little six-feet-under to get him out of these oppressive walls.

"Madam," the seer pleaded, "I don't understand." The seer was dragged in front of X and released with a fling that sprawled her face-first into the marble floor.

Saying nothing, Madame G stood over the seer in front of X, her arms crossed into the kimono sleeves. The same high ponytail of ink-black hair hung off the top of her head, and a calm, assessing façade was planted on her porcelain face. But X could sense her erratic breath and the fury roiling off her aura in waves.

The seer righted herself, surprising X by rising to her feet instead of remaining on her knees. She must have some level of esteem with Madame G not to be prostrate like a recruit. How long had she been held captive? Her clothes appeared used and worn, nothing more than a nightgown with a tie robe. Her light straw hair hung to her waist, and except for being used to drag the female across the room, looked well cared for and healthy.

"Seer," Madame G stepped forward and grabbed X's chin, nails digging into her jawbone, and jerked her face up, "tell me if I need to keep this traitorous failure alive."

X's eyes widened. She stared at Madame G, heeding her volatile demeanor. What if the seer shrugged her existence off? Should she take her chances now and attack Madame G? Was this the moment she'd been planning and yearning for, stabbing Madame G while she was somewhat distracted with her rage? Somehow, she thought her final battle would be more significant, not an underhanded last minute attempt.

Now is not your time.

Her gaze darted to the seer. X almost sent a questioning look to the older female, as if to ask, "Was that you? And are you talking about taking out the raging bitch in the room?" but she schooled her expression, waiting for the seer's response to Madame G's question.

"I see…I—I see…" The pale shifter stammered, her voice shaky, unlike the calming one that floated through X's mind.

"What?" Madame G nearly shouted. The air thinned in the room, like it was being sucked out as the female's temper rose. X had never personally witnessed Madame G lose her temper; they'd likely suffocate if she threw a tantrum. "What do you see?"

The seer took a cleansing inhale and turned her head slowly toward Madame G. "I do not see your success upon her death."

Madame G ripped her hand away from X's chin, causing her head to fling back, droplets of blood hitting the marble. She loomed over the seer, who didn't shrink back. The seer, X surmised, was used to the madam's outbursts.

"*You* told me to spare this pathetic creature when I killed her parents. That she would serve me well. Did you see her insubordination? Her treachery?"

This female was responsible for X's capture? That night ran through her mind. Dragging herself through mud made from dirt and blood, laughing Agents standing over her, kicking her so she stayed down. No eighteen-year-old girl, even a shifter female, could take on three trained fighters.

"Madame G," the seer replied in an even tone, like she had to repeat for the twelfth time to a five-year-old why they could not have chocolate for breakfast, "I obtain no visions of your enhanced Agents, only shifters. Hence why I can see your domination of our species. When I foresee your ascension over the shifters, I see Agent X at your back."

X didn't smell deceit from the seer, so were her words spoken true. Or was she blowing smoke up their mistress' kimono?

Your time will come. Persevere. The seer's voice drifted through her mind.

That totally didn't answer her question. Smoke rings or serving up the shifter species on a platter?

X came back with her own question. *Were you responsible for what happened to my family?* As in, did this female lead Sigma to her doorstep to slaughter her family because she saw X in a vision?

A flash of sadness answered X's question. *It was the only way to hide you.*

For what? Did you turn in E's family, too? Tell her they were with the Guardians? X challenged, trying to decide if she should hunt the seer down before she went after Madame G or, if she had any pulse left, *after* facing Madame G.

"Go back to your room." Madame G waved the seer off, centering on X, who went back to inspecting the floor in proper reverence.

Just...persevere, came the final message as the shifter scurried back through the hidden door.

So...don't die while I mettle in your life some more. And then what?

The next breath X took was devoid of air, choking her instantly. An invisible blow to the midsection dropped her to her knees as she gagged and gasped, searching for a scrap of oxygen. Be a good girl and don't attack the wicked witch. Be a good Agent and take your punishment, X thought to herself, the echo of the seer's words still in her mind. Could she trust the shifter? Would her time really come, and what would it bring?

The ding of the elevator brought two Agents who X couldn't sense while she was starved for air. The world dimmed and going unconscious around this place never ended well. One tended to wake up naked and defiled.

Before X's brain winked out for good, she heard Madame G's instructions to the Agents. "Teach her a lesson and let her think about it for a while."

Relief, cool and soothing, rushed through her even as she suffocated. The piñata treatment.

Oooh, even better. One of the Agents was a female. They'd delight in beating the sass out of X, but were less likely to try to teach her a sexual lesson and lord their dominance over the preferred Agent X. Most experienced Agents didn't try to mess with X's body. They knew there'd be a reckoning as soon as X was recovered and field ready. It also put them close to her and in a vulnerable position. And that had ended poorly for the last few who tried to use her body as their new toy.

Madame G released her hold on X's air supply, and as X swallowed in giant mouthfuls of stale indoor air, her sides were pummeled by heavily-booted feet. Locking the pain into a corner of her mind, she withstood the beating, pulling in lungfuls between kicks. It was standard to beat down an Agent so they had no fight left when hauled down for a "lesson." X would allow it to happen, knowing that even with the beating, she could overcome these two Agents and be back in her rooms in ten minutes.

Make it twenty. She would have to crawl back, but she'd get there.

Be a good girl, she reminded herself, spitting up mouthfuls of blood and wiping them off onto her shirt as they dragged her to the elevator to get to the lower levels. The less blood exposed to Madame G, the better. Her head pounded, her vision was hazy, and it felt like, well, like she'd been repeatedly kicked in the ribs. X was actually looking forward to the afterglow from the thrashing she was getting dragged to. While she was hanging out between beatings, maybe she could piece together all the new information dangled in front of her today. Persevere. She'd persevere the shit out of this punishment and make sure Madame G met her demise.

Epilogue

$\Longleftarrow\Sigma\zeta\Longrightarrow$

Commander Fitzsimmons was pacing. E couldn't help but think that was a bad thing. The male was always alarmingly still, quiet, observing his surroundings and the interactions between those around him. During the times E fought with the formidable Guardian leader, the male never wasted his movements. Once the commander uncoiled to strike, his hits were planned, precise.

Now, the grim commander was wearing a damn hole in the hardwood of his office with those black combat boots of his.

E's gut wrenched as he thought of how much the commander's actions reminded him of his partner. Old partner. Fuck. Friend? What was X to him? He'd never had a sister, no siblings, but X would be like if he had a brother and a sister all in one. They'd talk shit to each other, patch up the other's bullet holes, and then she'd ask if her hair was messed up, or if Sigma's leathers made her butt look big. Course she didn't care, but it wouldn't stop her from asking.

Back to the pacing commander. His restless energy was much like X's. She was always fiddling with something—her weapons, her hair, her nails. She never quit moving, whether it was walking a hole in the carpet, or moving her body to the beat of music only she could hear.

"You wanted to talk?" E finally broached the question because he'd been standing there almost ten minutes after the male had called him and told him to come to his office. He had arrived, nodded to the intense male, and then waited. And waited. The commander had ping-ponged off his office walls the entire time.

"We need to get her out." The pacing never slowed.

"Ooookay." E watched the commander, his concern no longer for what worked up the male, but for X. Because something was going on with her that was making the male distracted, distraught. "She stayed behind to finish the job we set out to do. I don't doubt she was punished for helping me and my family escape, but we've been through all of Madame's G's, I'ma-teach-you-a-lesson specials. X'll be okay."

A muscle flexed in the commander's jaw as he made a beeline to one wall, spun, and headed to the opposite wall; repeat. "Something's different. Something's not right."

E's concern started to smolder. He already felt cut off from the female who had been his only friend and family for the past ten years, having never been away from her that long. He felt like a guilty loser, too. Forming alliances and new friendships with the Guardians, going to sleep every night next to his mate after giving his son a hug good night and telling him to shut off the electronics, all this while X paid for his transgressions.

"Tell me what you know. I'll do anything to free her from Sigma and destroy Madame G. As long as Ana and Julio are safe, I'm in, man. I'm in."

The commander nodded absently, as if E wanting to help destroy Sigma was old news. It was, just not news a lot of people knew, and it humbled E to know the Guardians had embraced him and his family. Not only that, but kept him protected from their Lycan Council that wanted E's head on a stake. Commander Fitzsimmons had them mollified for now. Solemnly informing them that they were gathering all the information they could from the former Agent, and that it was imperative to have him close by when things with Sigma came to a boiling point.

The commander neglected to inform the council that E's mate was now enhanced like an Agent, and so was his son. The council didn't even know that Agents could mate. Instead, the clever bastard broached the topic as a hypothetical by saying, "We need to plan what we're going to do with subjects who were tested on and may no longer be completely human." And he did it in a way that gave the impression that killing innocent subjects would not be tolerated by the Guardians, no matter what the council's orders were.

The shifters had their hands full with the council, finding out if they were laced with corruption, possibly aiding Sigma or destroying their own to prevent them being used by Sigma. E did not envy the commander his position, but he would devoutly follow the male's authority, even though he would never be allowed to become a Guardian. As always, he would protect and serve.

"She's not there anymore." Commander Fitzsimmons' brows were drawn, he studied the floor. Even though E had a ton of questions about where the hell X would be, he kept his mouth shut, waiting. He didn't have to wait long. "I have an odd ability. I dream walk."

E's brows shot up. How handy would that be? What was the enemy planning? I don't know, let me peek in on him in his sleep, get him to gloat about his nefarious dealings.

"I don't use it much anymore. I can't get shit on Madame G and Agent's minds aren't normal." The commander looked at E and tapped his forehead. "Something's different up here, like you don't have normal dreams anymore and I can't get in. But once I found X, I started…" the male drifted off, his pacing speed increased until it took only a few strides before he had to turn again. "visiting her. Just, ya know, to check her out, see why I got paired with an Agent for a mate after all these years."

Just, ya know, to check her out. Riiiight. E suspected the male was as enraptured by X as his partner had been by him. And he didn't doubt the commander hid it as well as X had, until E finally confronted her about why she got all weird and girly after a confrontation with him. Or talked incessantly about when they'd face off again.

"She never mentioned anything." E didn't think they kept secrets from each other, but this one X never mentioned.

Commander Fitzsimmons shook his head. Pace and turn. Pace and turn. "I didn't even know if she knew it was me for years. We never talked, she never saw me. Just once and that was recently. I protected her sleep, so she could actually rest. The nightmares I walked into those first few times…" Again he drifted off. From his profile, the memories still distressed him.

"So she's not sleeping?" If she was dead, the commander would know. E would know. Right?

"She's not dead; I would know."

E blew a sigh of relief. Hearing the words meant more than he could imagine.

"But she's not sleeping. I can't mind-speak with her. So the only other reason would be she's injured so badly she can't function."

"It's been two weeks. It's not unheard of for punishment to last that long." E's mind raced. Did Madame G decide X wasn't worth keeping on the payroll?

"If she's been gone this long without her Agent X, it won't be much longer before Madame G elects to do without her permanently." The commander stopped dead center in front of E. The pain and angst in the male's eyes for his mate made E's emotions only a faint echo in comparison.

"The seer says X is destined to destroy Madame G." E offered, repeating what the commander had informed him earlier. "There's nothing to say that she has to be an Agent to do it. We need to get her out of there."

Sure, it would make getting back into the compound difficult, and getting close to Madame G impossible, but at least X would still be alive to *try*.

"Fuck Madame G and fuck X's destiny," the commander spit out. "She's my *mate*." Spoken like a shifter's mate and a vampire's true mate, since the male was a little of both. E knew exactly how the guy felt. The whole world could destroy itself, as long as he and Ana and Julio had a nice little corner to be left the hell alone.

But life didn't work out that way. The world threatened their loved ones, and once their mates were safe, then they could work on their quiet little corner. E's family was safe—for now. The commander's mate wasn't.

"I'll tell you everything I know about where she could be in the compound, what kind of torture she could be going through."

The commander cut his head to the left to glare at the wall, as if hearing his suspicions confirmed would be too much right now. E fell silent. "I can get that information. I have an inside source and I might even be able to trust him." The male's lip curled with the last statement, suggesting he despised the source and wanted a reason to distrust him.

E didn't bother asking who. If the commander wanted him to know, he would've said the name. "When do we go?"

PURE CLAIM
Book 5, The Sigma Menace

Alexandria King's life had been ripped away, destroyed by the evil organization Sigma, and one of its vilest leaders, Madame G. Alexandria was imprisoned, tortured, conditioned, and trained to become one of Sigma's finest Agents—Agent X. Except, despite what Sigma ordered, Agent X's only mission became keeping the secret of her bloodline, and using it to destroy Madame G. She's willing to sacrifice everything to carry it out, even her own chance at happiness with her destined mate.

Guardian Commander Rhys Fitzsimmons isn't willing to let the vivacious, frustrating female, who is supposed to be his mate, throw her life away, even for such a noble cause. When her single-minded mission almost destroys her before she can carry out her destiny, he breaks all the rules to save her. But her destiny is not as they were led to believe, and the real threat to their relationship is bigger than either of them could have known.

About the Author

Marie Johnston lives in the upper-Midwest with her husband, four kids, and an old cat. Deciding to trade in her lab coat for a laptop, she's writing down all the tales she's been making up in her head for years. An avid reader of paranormal romance, these are the stories hanging out and waiting to be told, between the demands of work, home, and the endless chauffeuring that comes with children.

Sign up for my newsletter at:
mariejohnstonwriter.com

Like me on Facebook

Twitter @mjohnstonwriter

Also by Marie Johnston

The Sigma Menace:
Fever Claim (Book 1)
Primal Claim (Book 2)
True Claim (Book 3)
Reclaim (Book 3.5)
Lawful Claim (Book 4)
Pure Claim (Book 5)

New Vampire Disorder:
Demetrius (Book 1)

Rourke (Book 2)

Pale Moonlight:
Birthright (Book 1)

.

Printed in Great Britain
by Amazon